Max Elliot Anderson

Big Rig Rustlers

DATE DUE

NOV 0 8			
OCT 1 2			
MAR 0 8			

Max Elliot Anderson

Big Rig Rustlers

Baker Trittin Press
Winona Lake, Indiana

Big Rig Rustlers
By Max Elliot Anderson

Printed in the United States of America
Cover Art: Paul S. Trittin

Published by Tweener Press Division
Baker Trittin Press
P.O. Box 277
Winona Lake, Indiana 46590

To order additional copies please call (574) 269-6100
or email info@btconcepts.com
http://www.gospelstoryteller.com

Publishers Cataloging-Publication Data
Anderson, Max Elliot
        Big Rig Rustlers - Tweener Press Adventure
Series / Max Elliot Anderson - Winona Lake, Indiana
Baker Trittin Press, 2004

                p.   cm.

Library of Congress Control Number: 2004110906
ISBN: 0-9752880-1-6
        1. Juvenile   2. Fiction   3. Religious   4. Christian
        I. Title   II. Big Rig Rustlers
JUV033010

Dedicated to
James Brightman

Chapter 1

"Family meeting!"

"Family meeting!"

Any time Todd heard those words, he knew it was something big, really big! Like the day he first found out they'd be moving to the new house, or when their dad brought home a new car.

We just got the new car two months ago, Todd thought, *so it can't be that.*

Todd might have been twelve-years-old, but he never got tired of hearing those exciting words, "Family meeting!"

"Family meeting!" his father called out again.

Todd scratched his head through the blond hair he liked to keep as short as possible. He blinked his dark blue eyes, then scrambled down the stairs as fast as he could. He jumped the last four steps and burst into the den all out of breath.

"What is it?" he asked.

"We have to wait till your sister gets here."

Just then, Amanda, Todd's ten-year-old sister, came

around the corner so fast she crashed right into half-blind, nearly deaf Stony, the family's english sheep dog. Whenever Stony heard, "Family meeting!" he tried his best to get there first, but he never made it. Stony had been part of the family even before Todd and Amanda. Todd's mother told him the dog was just one big kid himself.

Usually he was the last one to come bounding into the room, but this time Stony and Amanda got there at exactly the same time. They slammed into each other like two linemen on Monday Night Football and fell to the floor. One of Stony's paws got stuck in her blond ponytail. Amanda untangled her legs, arms, and hair from Stony's gangly legs and scurried to join the others.

"Good one, Mandy," Todd teased. He and his sister were good friends, always had been. That probably was because Amanda could take it just as well as give it out.

"I was just practicing how to flatten you in the back yard the next time we play football," she said.

"Only touch football," her mother reminded.

"Okay, Dad. Now what is it?" Todd begged.

"My friends . . . and my enemies." Todd's father always began his speeches to the family like that. "I call to order this special meeting of the Brannon family."

Todd already liked the sound of that, a special meeting.

"You remember your Uncle Reid?"

"Yeah, he has that big ranch out in Wyoming, doesn't he?"

"That's the one."

"What about him?"

"Well, your uncle has invited the two of you to visit the ranch during your spring break. Since you already get a week's vacation, we've arranged for an extra week from school. You have to do all your regular work, plus write a paper about your experiences. It should work out perfectly."

"What should work out?"

"He wants you to come for the spring roundup."

"I don't get it," Amanda said. "Who rounds up springs anyway?"

"You don't round up *springs*, Mandy. You round up cattle. We get to go out on a real western trail ride. Right Dad?"

"That's right. You will be camping out, and there will be a chuck wagon, horses, cowboys, and everything."

"Really?" Todd squealed. "This is so exciting! But Dad, how are we going to get there?"

"Your Uncle Reid has it all worked out. We'll take you to the airport and put you on a flight to Cheyenne, Wyoming. The airline will make sure you get where you need to go. It's already been arranged."

"When do we leave?" Amanda asked.

"This Saturday. The day after you get out of school. It's not much notice, but your mother and I thought it would be easier if you didn't have a lot of time to wait before you leave."

"Now we have a lot to do," their mother informed them. "I need to get your clothes all together, and you'll have to help pack your things. One suitcase each!"

The children ran back upstairs, "We're going to Wyoming. We're going to Wyoming!" They dashed to their rooms to start picking out what to pack.

The rest of the week went by very fast for Todd. He thought it might drag because he was so excited, but there was a lot to do at school before they had their break. He scarcely had time to think about the trip. Finally, Friday night came, and it was time to do the final packing.

Their mother bought each of them some extra jeans and shirts that were more rugged than their normal school clothes. After all, the school bus ride each day was not nearly as rough as the horseback riding they were expecting to do. Sleeping in their warm, soft, comfortable beds was much different than the campout conditions their father told them about.

"There's no way I'm going to get all this stuff into one suitcase," Amanda complained from her room across the hall. "Todd, you got any more room in yours?"

Todd walked into his sister's room, but he couldn't believe what he saw. Strewn all over her bed were matching outfits for every day of the week. On the chair she had six different jackets, and along the wall she had lined up at least eight pairs of shoes.

"Hey, Mandy. We're going to the wild, wild west not the White House. You've got way too much stuff here. Mom!" he yelled.

"What is it?" she called from the kitchen.

"Can you come up here a minute? Mandy needs some major help with all the junk she's trying to take."

When their mother came into the room, Todd saw the surprised look on her face. "Mandy . . . Sweetheart, you don't need *half* of these things."

"But Mom, I want to look nice every day."

"Believe me, after a couple days on a smelly horse, it won't matter. You'll look worse than you can imagine, and your clothes will look ten times worse."

"Ick. Now I'm not so sure I *want* to go."

"Be serious, Mandy. You're not going to a fashion show. Remember how everyone at school was so jealous of us?"

"I know, but you're a boy, and boys don't care how they look, especially when they go camping."

Amanda's mother helped her put several outfits back in the closet. "Just three pairs of shoes," her mother said.

"Only *three*? Which three? I can't decide."

"Tell you what," Todd said. "Give me that pad of paper on your desk." Amanda went over and got it.

"Bring a pen, too."

She handed them both to her brother.

"Now, I'm going to write the numbers from one to eight two times. I'll slip a number into eight of the shoes for your right foot. Then I'll take the other set of eight numbers and mix them up. All you have to do is pick the numbers out of my hands. first three you pick will be the three pairs of shoes that get to make the trip with you."

"This isn't fair. How could I ever decide?"

"I'm taking care of that problem by having the drawing."

11

"Oh, all right."

Todd proceeded to write out two sets of numbers. He placed the first set, one at a time, in the right shoe of each pair, but not in order. Then he folded the other eight pieces of paper and mixed them up in his cupped hands.

"Ready?" he asked.

"I guess so."

"Then draw." Todd tried to sound like a cowboy.

"Hey, quit it. You sound like one of those guys in the dumb old westerns Dad likes to watch."

"Well, draw anyway."

Amanda reached in with her trembling little fingers and began to lift out the first piece of paper. Then she dropped it back.

"I just *know* I won't like that one."

"How can you tell? That might have been your favorite pair."

"Todd, you're *not* helping!"

She reached in again, and this time pulled out the number seven. Amanda quickly ran over to see which one would be first.

"Oh, yuck. I hate that pair."

"Next."

This time she picked out the number four which turned out to be her favorite.

"Things are looking up," Todd said.

"As long as I have my favorite pair, I don't care what the third one is. Why don't you choose it?"

Todd reached with his other hand and picked out number five. When his sister found that one she yelled, "That's my second favorite. Thanks, Todd!"

"You're welcome."

"Can Mandy sleep in the extra bed in my room tonight?" Todd asked. "We might as well get used to it."

"I don't see why not," his mother answered.

"Just make sure you don't stay up half the night," their father warned from the doorway. "You're going to need your rest for the big trip ahead."

"We won't," they agreed.

By nine o'clock the two were snuggly in their beds. Then their parents came into the room for one last good night hug and kiss.

"We're very excited for you both," their dad told them. "I've been out to my brother's ranch a few times. I know you're gonna love it."

"We've only seen pictures, Dad. How big is it?" Todd asked.

"Last I heard it was around eighty thousand acres."

"Eighty thousand acres! That's almost more than our whole town. Why is it so big?"

"You'll see when you get there. The ranches in that area have to be big because not much grows out there. It isn't like the rich farmland we have around here. The cattle go out as far as they have to searching for food. Sometimes it takes days to find them all again. That's what the roundup is all about. You'll be going out to bring in all the new calves that have been born."

"Do we get to help?"

"*Get* to? On a ranch, everybody's expected to pitch in and work," Dad answered.

"Better get to sleep now, kids," their mother said. "I'm sure going to miss you two," she added with a slight crack in her voice.

Todd could see tears beginning to fill her eyes. She quickly turned and went into the hall as his father quietly shut the door. Try as they might, neither Amanda nor Todd was about to fall asleep anytime soon.

"Todd, have you ever ridden a real horse before?"

"Well, sort of. You have, too."

"Me? When?"

"Remember when we were both really small? We went on a pony ride at the county fair."

"Oh, that. The way those dinky little ponies were hooked together all they could do was walk around in a circle. Do you think it will be anything like that?"

"Nothing like that. Where we're going, if a horse decides to take off running and you don't know how to stop him, you might end up in Canada before he's finished with you. But you don't need to be scared, Mandy. I'm sure Uncle Reid will give us plenty of lessons."

"Do you think we'll have to ride big, man-sized horses?"

"Dunno. I guess you will just have to wait and see."

"Aren't there snakes out there, too?"

"Yup. Great *big* rattlesnakes."

"Yikes! What are we going to do?"

"Well, we won't be out there all by ourselves you know."

"I know. I'm sure glad I'll have you along. At a time like this, a big brother is a very good thing to have around." This was much kinder than she often talked about her brother.

"I'm glad you get to go, too. Uncle Reid must have waited till he thought you were old enough. I think you'll do okay."

"I sure hope so."

Chapter 2

Some time during the night Todd heard his sister calling, "Todd, help me. I fell off my horse."

"Fell off her horse? What in the world is she talking about?" he muttered barely awake.

Amanda kept calling. "I can't get up, Todd. My horse fell on me."

Todd himself was someplace between being totally unconscious and the uncertainty if it was real or just a dream. You know the feeling . . . when you'd rather pull the covers up over your head and go back to sleep. To make matters worse, it was still totally dark outside.

The faint glow from a streetlight, halfway down the block, gave just enough light to help Todd make out a few details in his room. Since the light also passed through the branches of a large maple tree outside his bedroom window, the shadows on his walls made all kinds of spooky shapes. It wasn't hard for Todd to imagine that there were outlaws and bad guys surrounding his bed.

He shuddered when he thought of some of the guys he hung out with. They'd started stealing a few things from a store near their school. But he'd never told anyone about it . . . not even Mandy.

His eyes adjusted better to the darkness, and he forgot about the guys at school. He blinked his eyes and by squinting he was able to just make out the other bed in his room, and his sister was definitely not in it.

"Mandy," he whispered, "where are you?"

All he could hear was the whimper of his little sister someplace in the dark. Todd could put up with a lot that his sister did, but there was one thing he couldn't tolerate. He hated to hear her cry, and right now she was crying.

"Mandy," he said a little louder, "it's me, Todd."

"I fell off my horse, Todd, and my clothes are all dirty. Help me."

Todd slithered out of his comfortable bed and began to feel his way around on the floor. He crawled along one side; no Mandy. Then he tried the end of the bed.

Not there either, he thought.

"Come on, Todd, I'm stuck in these bushes."

He tried the other side of the bed.

"Nope," he whispered. Then he thought he could hear her sniffing farther across the room. He flipped on a small reading light on the end table next to her bed, and then he saw the funniest thing. Well, it was funny to him. There, in his closet, was Mandy, all crumpled in a heap like a pile of laundry. Not only that, she was completely tangled up in her sheet and blanket that had been on top of her bed.

Todd once heard that sometimes when a person is sleepwalking or talking in their sleep, they aren't really aware of what is going on, but they talk anyway. That wouldn't be so bad except if another person talks to them, they usually answer even though what they say may make no sense at all. That's what Todd was facing.

"Mandy," he asked, "how did you get into my closet?"

"I'm not in the closet, silly. I'm over here in the bushes."

"Okay then, how did you get into the bushes?"

"I fell off my horse when he was trying to crawl under that fence back there."

"What fence?"

"That one," she said as she pointed straight up at the ceiling.

Todd couldn't resist going along with her. This was starting to get really good.

"Well, why did he want to go under the fence?"

"What fence?" she asked. "Oh, um, he was looking for his lunchbox."

That made Todd laugh right out loud, and when he did, his sister started to wake up.

"Hey, how did I get into your closet?"

"Never mind, buckaroo. Let's just get you back into . . . let's get you back on your horse."

"What horse?" she asked. "Are you crazy?"

Todd helped her get untangled, and then pulled her up on her feet. Gently he steered his sister back in the direction of her bed and made sure she got her head back on the pillow. He went back to the closet and retrieved her blanket. After covering Mandy with it, he tucked the blanket under both sides of the mattress. No more sleep walking tonight!

Todd climbed into his own bed, but by now he was wide-awake.

Todd loved Amanda a lot. He remembered the day she came home from the hospital. He was home with his grandmother when the garage door opened, and his parents brought her into the house.

It was exciting to see a new baby, even if it was a girl. His parents had let him help get the room ready for the new baby. That made Todd feel pretty important. A protective feeling began that day and never stopped. After all, she was a *little* sister.

He'd heard some of his friends talk about how much they hated their younger brothers or sisters, but those feelings never found a place in Todd's mind. *I hope nothing bad ever happens to Mandy,* he thought. *I don't know what I would do without her.* As he drifted off to sleep, he decided there wasn't anything he wouldn't do for her.

The next thing he knew, his father was tapping him on the shoulder, "Todd. It's time to get up."

"So soon?"

"Don't you remember? We have to get to the airport extra early so we can get you checked in for your flight."

"It's just that I didn't get much sleep, that's all."

"Too excited about your trip? Well, that's to be expected."

"Not exactly." He looked over to his sister and noticed that she was sleeping like a baby. It didn't seem fair because, actually, she had slept through the whole night.

Todd showered first, so he was almost finished with breakfast when his sister finally came downstairs.

"Boy, Mom, my shoulder is really sore."

"Did you sleep the wrong way on it last night?"

"I don't know. Must have. How bout you, Todd? Did you sleep okay?" she asked.

"Oh, I guess so, except when I had to help you back up on your horse."

"Huh?"

"Never mind. You'd better hurry up and eat so we can load our stuff in the car and get going."

Their father was already out in the garage making room in the trunk. He usually kept his golf clubs in there along with some stuff that belonged to Todd and Amanda, things they weren't going to need in Wyoming.

Before long he came into the kitchen. "Are you both about ready?"

"Not quite," Todd answered. Amanda didn't say anything. Todd took one look at her, and it was plain to see she was still pretty sleepy.

"Let's circle the wagons," their father announced. That always meant it was time to go. He loved to use western talk.

Too bad he didn't live on a ranch.

The children rushed upstairs to brush their teeth, and cram a few last minute things into their bags, before heading toward the car.

"Hey, this thing is too heavy," Amanda complained. "I can't carry it, Todd."

"I'm not surprised. You have half the mall in there."

"C'mon, Todd. Would you help me?" she pleaded.

"Oh, all right, but let me take mine down to the car first. Then I'll come back up for yours."

As he pulled his suitcase down the stairs behind him, it hit every step with the rhythm of a big base drum . . . boom, boom, boom, boom!

"Todd," his mother yelled, "could you pick that thing up, *please?*"

"Sorry, Mom, but it's too heavy."

"Are you sure you need all those things?"

"This is nothin'. Wait till I drag Mandy's bag down. You'll probably have to call someone to come and build new steps after I wind up crashing clear through to the basement."

"When you get to the garage, ask your father to go up and get it."

"Okay. I'll be glad to."

When Todd came back into the kitchen, he heard boom, boom, boom, boom, coming from the stairs.

"Honestly," his mother said in disgust as she picked up her purse. "Sometimes the men in this family. . . ."

Todd wasn't sure what she meant by that, but the tone of her voice made him decide it was better if he didn't ask.

Soon the family was on their way to the airport. It would only take an hour and a half to get there. Todd looked at his watch and decided they had plenty of time to make their flight. He was excited because this was only his third trip on an airplane. The other two times they had traveled as a family, but this time he had to be in charge. He was a little nervous, but only a little.

"There's a lot of traffic for this time on a Saturday morning," Todd's father complained. "What's the deal?"

"It might be because everyone else is on spring break, too," their mother suggested.

"Sure, that's probably it. We should have left a lot earlier."

After a few minutes, Todd's mother and sister were sound asleep as the car headed toward the beginning of the greatest adventure Todd and Mandy could ever imagine. Todd couldn't sleep. He was still tired, but he couldn't help thinking about the trip.

He remembered the old album in the family room. Todd had seen several pictures from Uncle Reid's ranch. He often wondered what life would be like in the wild, wild west.

There were pictures showing cattle as far as the pictures could show. There were cowboys, too, real live cowboys on horses with ropes, big cowboy hats, boots, and everything. Todd remembered how rugged the land looked. There were rocks and canyons all over his uncle's ranch. He had looked at the thick brush in the pictures and wondered if it was easy to get lost out there.

Pictures of rattlesnakes always scared him. In one picture Todd saw a snake with its mouth wide open and the fangs sticking out. Even though he was sitting in the back seat of the car now, remembering that picture sent a cold chill through his entire body. For just a few seconds, he shivered a little. His father noticed that.

"Need me to turn on the heat?" his father asked.

"No, thanks, I'm okay."

Snakes. There wasn't anything else in the whole world that scared Todd more than snakes. He wasn't sure why because he'd always thought girls were supposed to be afraid of them. *Mom is scared to death of snakes*, he thought.

"Are you afraid of snakes?" he asked his father.

"Not really. I've always been kind of fascinated by them," he answered.

"Why are some people afraid?"

"It goes back to Adam and Eve, I guess. Actually, snakes are quite beautiful, and they usually won't bother you if you don't bother them."

"Well," Todd replied, "whenever I see one of those National Geographic specials about Pythons, or Cobras . . . man, Cobras really bother me with that big head that just pops up out of the grass. I'm sure glad we don't live in India. I couldn't take having those things around, and I think Stony would have a heart attack if he ever saw one."

"There's the sign for the airport. Wake up everyone."

Todd's father pulled into the short-term parking lot. He rolled down his window, punched a green button on the machine, and out popped a ticket. Then the gate went up automatically. They drove through and found a parking spot.

The suitcases had wheels, and each had a handle that pulled out so they could be dragged like little trailers. The family walked toward a small building where they would get on a shuttle train that went from the parking lot to all the airline terminals. The doors to the building opened automatically, like at the grocery store, and they headed toward the escalator. When they reached the top, other people were standing there waiting for the train, too.

"I can already hear some of the jets, Dad," Todd said excitedly. "Man, I just love the smell of jet fuel."

A voice came over a big speaker, "The train is entering the station. Please step back." It came to a stop, and its doors opened. Todd looked around, but he couldn't see anyone operating the train.

"Who's runnin' this thing?" he asked.

"It's all done by computer. The program tells it when to stop, when to go, how fast, and when to open the doors."

Soon they were slowing in front of their terminal building. The doors opened, and Todd's father said, "This is us. Everybody out."

Todd looked out onto a sea of people waiting in long lines. "We're never going to get through this mess," he complained.

"Sure you will," his mother reassured him.

"I'm so excited," Amanda squealed. She reached up and hugged herself, swinging her shoulders back and forth.

"Why do you do that, Mandy?" Todd asked. "People are watching you."

"I can't help it, and besides, I don't care. These people don't know me, and I sure don't know them."

A woman in a dark uniform, with a clipboard in her hands and a tag with her name and picture on it, walked up and asked, "Are you Todd and Amanda?"

Todd and his sister had been warned about talking to strangers, and he'd never seen this woman before so they didn't answer.

"Yes, they are," Todd's father told her.

"We've been waiting for you. Everything has been arranged. You're going to have a wonderful time."

It wasn't long before their flight was announced. Todd and Amanda hugged and kissed their mother and told her goodbye. Then their dad went with them and the lady as they boarded the plane.

Chapter 3

"I have to actually put you in your seats. Then they make me get off the plane," Todd's father told the children.

"Why don't you just stay on with us? Who would know?" Amanda asked.

"They count the passengers, Amanda. They count all of them. What would Mom think if I did that?"

Amanda giggled. "I didn't think about that."

The plane wasn't a big one. It had only two jet engines, one on each wing. There were three seats on one side and just two on the other. Todd and Amanda had seats 24D and E. Todd let his sister have the window seat so she could look outside during the flight. Their father gave them each a hug before he left the plane.

"Good," Todd said.

"What's good?"

"Only two seats on our side. Now we won't have to sit with anyone else."

"So what?"

"Do you want to spend the next two hours listening to

someone say, 'My, aren't we all grown up flying by ourselves. And where are we going today?'"

"Oh, yeah. That wouldn't be much fun. Do we get anything to eat on our flight?" Amanda asked.

"Dad said we don't. That's why mom packed a lunch. I have it in my backpack. But we *are* supposed to get something to drink."

"Well, I'm already starving."

"Me, too, Starvin' Marvin."

A flight attendant stopped by to make sure the children had their seatbelts fastened. "After the plane lands in Cheyenne, you just stay in your seats. I'll come back and walk you out to the terminal."

"Okay," Todd answered.

The flight was nearly full, so it took a few more minutes before everyone was seated. Someone closed the front door, and Todd could hear the engines start. After that, he felt something push from the front of the plane as they began moving backward away from the building..

"I'm really excited, Todd. I was too small to remember the last time we flew."

Their plane began turning to the left, the engines sounded a little louder, and they moved forward.

"Good morning, ladies and gentlemen. This is your captain speaking. I'd like to welcome you on our flight to Cheyenne this morning. Our flying time should be about two hours and forty minutes. We'll be flying at an altitude of thirty thousand feet. Weather this morning looks clear, but other pilots have reported upper air turbulence. So, we'd like to ask you to keep your seatbelts fastened throughout the flight. For now, you can just sit back and enjoy the ride."

"He sounds like a nice man," Amanda said. "I wonder if he has kids?"

"I have *no* idea."

The plane continued to taxi toward the runway at a slow, lumbering speed.

"This is your captain again. The tower tells us we're the next in line. We expect an on-time arrival in Cheyenne. Thank you for flying with us today."

Their plane came to a stop. Todd wondered if something was wrong, but then the engines got louder again as they made a right hand turn. This time they didn't stop. Instead, the engines roared to life as the plane began thundering down the runway. Soon they were in the air.

"Look at those cars, Todd. They look like some of your toys back home."

"Yeah, and the people look like they live in your ant farm."

After only a few minutes, they flew into a layer of clouds.

"Hey, I can't see anything," Mandy complained. No sooner had she said that than the plane came out the other side.

"Todd, look out there. It looks like a bunch of cotton."

"Marshmallows would be more like it."

Mandy smacked her lips, "Mmm, I love marshmallows."

A woman's voice came over the speakers. "We're going to

begin serving in a few minutes. If you would like something to drink, please put your tray tables down."

They quickly lowered the table in place and waited. When the flight attendant came to their row, each chose a cola, and a tiny package of chips was served with it.

Later their flight attendant came by and took away all the trash. Todd and his sister put the tray tables back up so they could have more room.

"Do you want to play something?" Todd asked.

"No, thanks."

"Like a book or anything?"

"I don't think so. I'm going to try to sleep."

Todd looked around and noticed that many of the other passengers were already sleeping.

"That sounds pretty good to me, too, but I'm going to read my book for awhile."

He was glad to get a couple weeks away from the troublemakers he'd been stealing with at school. Todd didn't feel good about the stealing, but he was trying to fit in. The guys he ran with were some of the most popular in his grade at school.

Todd's sister not only walked in her sleep sometimes, she was also a person who fell asleep right away. Just then he felt her head bump into his shoulder. He looked over to see Amanda already conked out. He really felt a responsibility for his younger sister.

Todd was kind of proud of himself. Here he was, trusted by his parents to take care of things. He didn't even need to sleep. He opened the library book he'd checked out, *Rustlers of the Old West*. He wanted to know as much as possible so he wouldn't look stupid on the cattle drive.

"One of the most famous people who ever rustled cattle was Butch Cassidy," the book began, "but he found the work too hard and the profits too little. That's why he turned to robbing banks and trains."

Todd started wondering if there were cattle rustlers today. He'd never heard of any except in stories and movies about the Old West.

That'd be scary on our roundup, he thought.

The next thing he heard was the captain instructing the flight attendants to prepare for landing. It was immediately followed by Amanda shaking him and saying, "Todd, wake up. We're landing." Todd was a little embarrassed that he had nodded off to sleep, but he acted like everything was just fine.

The kids stuffed things back into their backpacks as the flight attendants walked up the aisle collecting any last minute trash. Todd saw them push some of the seats back up even though the people were still sleeping in them.

There were two small bumps, and then the engines roared louder than before as the pilot hit the brakes to bring his plane to a grinding stop. Then he revved the engines again and made a left turn.

"Ladies and gentlemen," a woman's voice began. "Welcome to Cheyenne, Wyoming, where the time is three twenty-five. Make sure to change your watches. We want to thank you for flying with us today and look forward to seeing you again."

"Do we get the same people when we fly back home?" Amanda asked.

"I doubt it."

"Why not?"

"It's too complicated to explain right now, Mandy."

Soon their plane taxied to its gate at the terminal, stopped, and the engines turned off. A bell sounded, and suddenly everyone stood up to begin getting out. Todd remembered that he and his sister had to wait.

"Do you remember what Uncle Reid looks like?" Amanda asked.

"Sort of. He'll probably have on a cowboy hat, boots, jeans . . . stuff like that."

"You mean like half the guys on this plane?"

"Here. Dad gave me a picture, and I think he's supposed to be holding up a sign. Besides, the flight lady will help us find him."

After most of the people from the back of the plane had moved toward the exit, the flight attendant came to Todd and asked, "Are you ready now?"

"We sure are," he said.

They grabbed their backpacks, walked single-file, and went out the door of the plane into a long hallway. At the end of it was a wide door. As soon as they walked through it, they saw a big, tall man with an even bigger smile on his face. He wouldn't have needed any sign. Todd knew right away it was Uncle Reid.

If you looked up the word "cowboy" in the dictionary it should say, "See Todd's uncle." He wore a wide, white cowboy hat. His western checked shirt and blue jeans went perfectly with his shiny black cowboy boots. His deep reddish-brown skin looked like he'd been out in the hot sun for a very long time.

"Hey, kids!" the man yelled, "it's good to see you." They ran together and he hugged each of them with one of his strong arms. Uncle Reid squeezed them so hard he lifted them right off the ground. Then he swung them around and said, "This here is your Aunt Debbie, but I just call her Darlin'."

Their aunt looked like a picture you'd find in a Wyoming fashion magazine. Her dark brown hair touched her shoulders, but she didn't wear a hat or boots. Other than that, she was dressed just like a cowgirl.

"Todd, Amanda, you have grown at least two feet since I saw you last."

"No, I already had two feet when you were at my house," Amanda protested. "I saw the pictures." Then everyone laughed.

"Are we close to your ranch now?"

"No sireee," his uncle laughed again. "We still have to drive over three hundred miles. It's big open country out here in Wyoming. Nothin' is close to nothin'."

After they found their suitcases in baggage claim, Uncle Reid said, "Wait here. I'll go get the truck."

Truck? Todd thought. *I wonder if we have to ride in the back of his dirty pickup?*

A few minutes later a large green truck pulled up in front.

33

It had double tires on the back, and more lights than Todd had ever seen on a truck before . . . even more than on a fire truck. At first Todd wasn't sure if this was the one or not, but then his uncle climbed out of the cab. It wasn't exactly a truck after all. It looked like one of those long limos Todd had seen at the airport back home. The only difference is this one had mud splattered all down the sides. Todd could see where the windshield wipers had cut their pattern through what otherwise would have been nothing but more mud. He couldn't tell if the truck had hubcaps or not, but he did like the way its engine rumbled. Todd thought it sounded like one of those powerful, road-eating monster trucks he'd seen on TV.

"Well, get in," their uncle told them as he grabbed the bags and tossed them in the back. Aunt Debbie waited for the kids to climb in and get settled in the back seat before she got in and closed the door. Uncle Reid climbed behind the wheel, put on his seatbelt, slapped into gear, hit the gas, and they roared away.

Todd began thinking about the adventures ahead. The plane trip already had given its share of excitement, but somehow, he thought the ranch, horses, and the roundup with a chuck wagon were going to be a lot of fun. Still, he couldn't get the idea of rustlers out of his mind.

Chapter 4

"Hey," Todd said, "I thought we were going to meet our cousin when we got to the airport."

"Drew wanted to come, but he was more interested in getting the bunkhouse ready for you."

"What's a bunkhouse?" Amanda asked.

"It's where all the cowboys sleep," Todd told her.

"You mean I have to sleep in a room with a bunch of cowboys that smell like horses and cows?" she protested.

Uncle Reid put his nose in the air and took a long, deep sniff, "Where I come from, there isn't a sweeter smell than cows and horses."

Amanda just wrinkled up her face and pinched her nose. "Not where I come from," she said with a funny sound.

"No, sweetheart," her Aunt Debbie comforted. "I think you'll be pleasantly surprised when you see it."

It didn't take long before their SUV was streaking down the Interstate. Their uncle kept trying to make the trip interesting even though the countryside looked pretty rough to

Todd. It was beautiful, with mountains in the distance, but Wyoming could be best described as a wide-open place.

"We pass by places with some interesting names," Uncle Reid announced.

"Like what?" Amanda asked.

"Let me see. Horse Creek, Sheep Mountain, Lost Springs, and Thunder Basin are just a few of them. Well, the truth is, once we get off this Interstate and travel up old 59, there aren't many places to see. But we do come close to a little town called Casper."

Amanda giggled, "Casper. That's such a cute name."

"Uncle Reid, do we go anywhere near Devil's Tower?" Todd asked.

"Why do you want to know about that place?"

"Last year in our geography class we all got to pick a state. We had to do research, make maps, and write a report. But the most interesting part of the assignment was building a model."

"Did you make a model of Devil's Tower?"

"Another boy had Wyoming, but he said in his report that it was the first National Monument in America. Is that true?"

"Yes, it is. Only I wish they could come up with a better name for it besides Devil's Tower because it's such a beautiful place."

"Well, his report said it's where some Native American Indians worshipped or something."

"That's true."

"Do we drive near it on the way to your place?" Amanda

asked.

"No, we don't, but it isn't too far from our ranch. I think we can find a way to go see it."

"Could we?" Todd exclaimed.

Uncle Reid nodded indicating it could be done. Then he leaned forward to turn on the radio.

The kids quickly learned that one thing Uncle Reid and Aunt Debbie liked a lot was Country Gospel Music. Not only did they like it, they liked it good and loud. Uncle Reid had a special sound system installed in his truck with speakers all over the place. No matter where a person sat, there was no escaping the music.

Todd leaned over and whispered to Amanda, "I feel like we have front row seats."

"What do you mean, where do we eat?" she blurted.

"Are you children hungry?" their aunt asked.

"No, thank you, not yet," Todd said with a grin. Even with the loud music, both children began having a battle with their eyelids. Todd felt like both of his had lead weights like fishermen use. As hard as he tried to keep his eyes open, it seemed they tried harder to slam shut. Finally, they did. When Todd woke up again, he looked over to see his sister still sleeping. He also noticed that it had gotten dark outside. When he looked out the front window, he could see that they were no longer on a beautiful, smooth, four-lane Interstate. Just as his eyes were adjusting, Uncle Reid yelled, "Whoa!" At the same time he slammed on his brakes and came sliding to a stop like one of those NASCAR race drivers making a panic pit stop.

"What?" Todd gasped.

Amanda sat straight up in her seat. "Are we there yet?" she said sleepily.

"Not yet, but we almost made hamburger out of that bull up there," Uncle Reid answered.

Todd squinted his eyes but still didn't see anything. "Where?" he asked.

His uncle turned up the high beams on his truck, and flipped on another set of four lights on the roof. Then, Todd saw it for sure. There, right in the middle of the road, stood one of the biggest animals he had ever seen.

"We best drive around him because I don't think he's gonna move any time soon."

"Where did he come from?"

"There might be a broken fence 'round here some place. We've also been hearing reports that rustlers are working this area again."

"Rustlers must be pretty dumb if they left a big guy like that behind," Amanda said.

"It might look that way, but now days those guys move pretty fast. They may have broken down a fence or gate, stolen what they could see, and high-tailed it out of here. There's some rustling in broad daylight, but most of it happens at night. That ol' boy could have been standing nearby, and they just missed him. Then, after they left, he might have gone out looking for his friends."

"That's so sad," Amanda said with a crackling voice.

Uncle Reid picked up a microphone that was attached to his dashboard and said, "Base, this is Reid Rider. Over."

A few seconds passed and a voice on the radio responded, "Reid Rider, this is base. Come back."

"Hey, Travis, is that you?"

"Yes, sir, Mr. Brannon. Over."

"I'm Northbound on 59 about ten miles south of the 387 junction near Thunder Basin."

"So what's up, sir?"

"Well, we just missed mowing down one of the finest hunks of beef I've ever seen around these parts. He was smack in the middle of the road."

"What do you want me to do, sir?" the voice asked.

"Get on the horn and call Sheriff Jackson. He'll know what to do."

"Yes, sir. What do you think? Rustlers?"

"Affirmative."

"That doesn't sound good. I'll get right on it."

"Thanks, and tell Drew to stay up till we get there."

"No problem. He said there was no way he was going to bed before the. . . . "

"What was that? You broke up."

"No, I didn't. I just decided to . . . are they in the truck with you now?"

"Yes, they are."

"Drew's right here. You want to talk to him?"

"Put him on."

"Hey, Dad. Whatcha want?"

"Remember what we talked about?"

"Yup, why?"

"Just checking. We won't be too long now."

"Okay. Here's Travis."

"I called the Sheriff, Mr. Brannon. He's going to send some of the boys out there to check it out in the morning and talk to the rancher. He said he'll give you a call sometime later tomorrow."

"Sounds good to me. I'm gone."

"Out," Travis said.

Todd looked at Amanda. He could tell she felt the same way he did just by the look on her face. He wondered if they might see real cattle rustlers.

This trip to Wyoming was going to be one adventure after another. He knew it would be nothing like the sleepy little street they lived on back home where the most exciting thing that ever happened was an occasional ambulance with its flashing lights and blaring siren in the middle of the night.

Ever since Todd had awakened from his nap he realized he hadn't seen the lights from a single car, truck, or anything. *We really are out in the middle of nowhere*, he thought.

"Uncle Reid. Doesn't anybody else besides you live out here?" he asked.

"Sure. Why?"

"Because I don't see houses, towns, cars. Nothin'."

"That's because we need a lot of land for our horses and cattle to find food. Ranches out here can be thousands and thousands of acres, but most of it's scrub brush and rocks."

Suddenly, all four tires locked up as the truck began sliding to one side again.

"That *idiot*. He doesn't even have his lights on!"

Todd could just make out the shape of a trailer of some kind moving slowly in front of them.

Their uncle grabbed his radio again and shouted, "Base, base, this is Reid Rider! Take this information down and relay it to the sheriff . . . Wyoming plate number, KAF-1520."

"Are they trying to be funny with the KAF?" Travis asked.

"What do you mean?"

"It sounds like calf."

"I don't know, but it's a truck and trailer out here being driven with its lights off. Makes me a little suspicious. I'm not sure if there is anything going on here, but at least the sheriff will have the information. Out."

With that Uncle Reid swung his truck into the passing lane and powered past the truck and trailer. As soon as he got around, the driver behind him turned on his bright lights and began speeding up.

In a voice filled with worry Todd asked, "What's he doing?"

"Never mind. He can't keep up with us pulling that heavy load behind his pickup."

Soon they were far enough away that Amanda uncovered

her eyes, "Are they gone yet?" she asked.

"Don't worry, honey," Aunt Debbie comforted. "Your big, strong Uncle Reid won't let anything happen to you."

Todd's earlier excitement turned to all-out fear. He began wondering if it was such a good idea to come out here after all. Stories he had heard about the wild west now didn't seem so far out to him. He sank slowly into his seat.

This is only the first night and already we almost hit a bull and probably saw some real live rustlers, he thought. That put a quivering feeling deep down in his stomach.

Chapter 5

After they'd driven a little farther, Todd spoke, "Uncle Reid?"

"Yes."

"Did the people with covered wagons travel at night like we are?"

"No, that would be much too dangerous."

"Too dangerous? What do you call this trip then?"

His uncle chuckled, "You might not believe it, but tonight has been a little unusual. It must be some kind of a wicked Wyoming welcome for you."

"I'll say. How much farther is it to your ranch?"

"About an hour now."

Before the bull in the road and the rustlers, Todd's aunt had passed out lunches she'd made. Todd and his sister had peanut butter and honey sandwiches, a banana, sugar cookies, and a juice box. But that was long enough ago that he was getting hungry again. He hoped there would be something to eat at the bunkhouse.

It didn't seem all that long until the truck slowed and the turn signal started blinking. Todd thought that was pretty funny. "Who are you signaling to, jackrabbits?" he laughed.

"It's just a habit I guess. There she is. The Double R Ranch."

As they turned into a dusty single lane, Todd saw a huge wooden gate with massive high posts on each side. Across the top was an even bigger sign that had "RR" on it. Todd decided it must stand for Reid Rider since he'd heard that name on the radio. But he still didn't see any lights, or buildings, or anything.

"Where *is* your place?" he asked.

"We're on it right now. It takes about twenty minutes to drive in to the main ranch."

"Wow, it must be really big," Amanda gulped.

Then it happened. The truck drove up a steep hill, came to a level spot, and started down the other side. That's when Todd and his sister saw more lights than they had seen for the past several hours. There were big buildings all around, a huge house, and rugged wooden fences everywhere.

Todd let out a long, loud whistle, "Big isn't a big enough word for this place."

The truck began to drive around a large circle in the dirt road until it came to a long, green building with a sign out front that said, "Bunkhouse."

"This is it, your new home for the next couple weeks."

Todd wasn't sure what the inside would be like, but he was already pretty impressed by the outside. With the light from the yard lights perched high on more wooden poles, he could see the bunkhouse was as nice as some of the houses in his neighborhood back home. He hadn't expected to see anything quite like it way out here. He had pictured a place with no paint, loose, weathered boards, broken down steps and doors with no screens.

"This looks great," he said.

"Wait till you see the inside," his aunt added.

Just then a rugged-looking boy came walking out onto the porch. He looked like he'd been chiseled out of the same jagged rock as Uncle Reid. To Todd he was almost a copy of his uncle, only smaller. Drew could as easily have been named, "Little-Me" by his father. He even walked with the same slow saunter as Todd's uncle. Then, it hit him.

"Is that Drew?" he asked.

"Sure is," his uncle said as he opened the truck door. "Hey, you little tumbleweed, come on over here and meet your cousins."

The boy came closer. The lights from inside the truck gave him a glimpse of the two strangers.

"Hey," he said.

"Hey, yourself," Todd answered.

"Todd, Amanda," Uncle Reid said, "this is your cousin Drew."

"Howdy," he mumbled.

"So, Drew, grab some stuff in the back and we can show them to their rooms."

"Rooms? We each have our own room?" Amanda asked.

"Unless you want to stay together in the same one," her aunt said.

"Oh, no, that's okay. But where do all the smelly cowboys sleep?"

"What smelly cowboys?" Drew asked.

"Never mind, Drew," his mother scolded. "The rest of the ranch hands have their own big place on the other side of the corral. You can see it tomorrow. Come on now. Let's go inside and get you settled. We have a big day tomorrow."

Drew jammed his hands deeper into his pockets and scoffed, "They're all big out here."

"Pick up some things, son," his father ordered.

The children walked up the steps first then waited by the door. Their aunt reached out and opened the door for them. As they entered the living room, Todd blinked in amazement. The room was cow everything. The furniture was made of leather and light-colored wood. On the walls were paintings of cowboys with cattle, cowboys roping calves, cattle stampeding, and cattle just standing around. The curtains, rugs, and pillows were all made out of cow skins. Todd looked over at one of the lamps and noticed that it was the leg from a real cow. The hoof was the part that made the lamp stand flat on the table. He pointed that out to his sister.

"Yikes! That gives me a creepy feeling," she said. "Where's the rest of him?"

Above all the doors they saw a full set of horns that used

to sit on the head of a real animal.

"Come on, I'll show you your rooms," Drew announced with pride. He first took them to Amanda's room. When he swung open the door, she screamed, "I get to stay in here?"

"Yes, this is for you. Is it okay?" her aunt asked in a worried voice.

"Is it okay? Is it okay? Are you kidding? This is the most beautiful room I've ever seen."

It was decorated with frilly curtains, a canopy bed with pink checked material on top that matched the curtains, a comforter that also matched, along with matching pillowcases and sheets. Everything was done in soft green and pink.

"I LOVE this room."

Her aunt showed her that she had her own bathroom, TV, and a bookcase with lots of books a girl would like to read.

"Come on, Todd, let me show you your room," Drew offered. He took Todd across the hall and opened that door.

"Now this is more like it," Todd said. His eyes gazed into a room that looked like the inside of an old mine shaft. The bed was made out of a mine car. The blankets and pillowcases looked like old sacks, and the windows didn't have curtains. His windows had big wooden shutters he had to close at night from the inside if he wanted it still dark in there by morning.

"Here," Drew added, "this is the best part." He walked over to the wall and started flipping switches. The lights in the room became very dim, and Todd was sure he could hear voices and the sounds of hammers hitting rock.

"That sounds just like miners working in here."

"Jump in your bed. I'll show you something else."

Todd climbed up into the mine car and his cousin pushed another button. The car started to rock back and forth as the sound of clicking tracks came from underneath him.

"I've never seen anything as neat as this in my whole life. Hey, Mandy. You gotta see this."

His sister came into the room, and stopped just inside the door. "Wow," she said as her mouth dropped open. "Can we switch?"

"There is no way I'm sleeping in a room that looks like it was made for Little Bo Peep. I can tell you that right now. This is a man's room, and I'm stayin'."

"Okay, Drew. We need to let the cousins get settled. There's food in the kitchen so you can help yourselves to anything you like. But remember, just like back home, brush your teeth, and don't stay up too late. Breakfast is at seven."

"Seven o'clock in the morning?" Amanda complained.

"We cram a lot into our days out here on the ranch. Tomorrow, Drew can show you around the place."

"I can't wait," Todd exclaimed as he rubbed his hands together.

His aunt, uncle, and cousin left the bunkhouse, and the children walked into the kitchen to see what there was to eat. Todd found the cupboards and refrigerator stocked with everything they could possibly want. It wasn't hard to pick out some grapes, cheese and crackers, granola bars, and juice.

Todd and his sister sat at the table gobbling all the goodies they'd found.

"Hey, Mandy," he asked, "what do you think of our cousin?"

"I think I kinda like him. Why?"

"He seemed to be trying to make us out to be stupid or something. I don't know why."

"Well, does he have any other brothers or sisters?"

"I don't think so."

"Then that's probably it."

"What's it?"

"He doesn't have a sweet, adorable, lovable, darling, perfect, little sister to keep him in line like you have."

That made Todd laugh. "Oh, you think you've got something to do with what a strong, great, kind, handsome, wonderful, big brother I am?"

"What do you mean by handsome?" Then they both laughed.

"We need to hit the hay so we're rested in the morning," Todd said.

"Okay. But can we sleep with our doors open in case I need you for something in the night?"

"Need me? You've never needed me at home."

"I know. But out here I think I'd just feel a little better, that's all."

"Are you afraid of something?"

"Not really. Except those guys with the trailer scared me

something awful."

"Me. too."

"They did?"

"Yeah. I thought they were going to try to run us off the road. Then there's no telling what might have happened."

"Do you think they had guns?"

"Let's not talk about it. Okay?"

"Okay."

The children brushed their teeth like they had been reminded, and soon each was snugly tucked in bed. The lights were out, but light still spilled in through the windows from the powerful spotlights outside.

"Hey, Todd. How come they have so many lights out there?"

"Do you really want me to tell you what I think?"

"Sure. Why?"

"Because I think it's to keep those bad guys from sneaking in here and stealing some of the animals."

"Really?"

"Really."

The next thing Todd heard was the pounding of his sister's little feet as she ran into his room like a wide receiver. She took one big leap, and landed up in his bed.

"Can I sleep in here tonight?" she begged.

"No way. This little cart is just big enough for one."

"Would you at least take me back to my room and wait till I'm asleep then?"

"Oh, all right."

He took his little sister into her room, and lucky for him, she conked right out like she always did. Once he was sure she was out cold, he went back to his room. He wasn't all that thrilled about being the bigger, stronger brother. Right now he wouldn't have minded someone a little bigger and a little stronger in the next room that *he* could depend on.

Todd lay down in his bed and pulled the covers up to this chin. He thought for a moment, and then yanked them clear over his head.

"I sure hope this place isn't dangerous," he whispered as he drifted slowly off to sleep.

Chapter 6

Todd awakened early the next morning. It wasn't because there was a lot of noise. Quite the opposite.

This place is so quiet it's kinda spooky, he thought. As he slipped out of his covers, his feet made a slapping noise on the hardwood floors. It was like the sound he remembered seals making at the zoo when they wanted their trainer to throw them some fish. The thought of those cute critters made him smile. Then, the more he heard his feet on the floor, slap,slap,slap,slap, the more he began to laugh, louder and louder. Between the slapping and the laughing, he woke his sister.

"Hey, what's so funny?"

"I was thinking of how my feet sound just like a seal begging for food." Then he threw his head back and barked, "Arf, arf, arf," as he clapped his hands together.

"I'm going to throw you something bigger than a fish if you don't cut that out," his sister threatened.

They heard the front door open, and then quickly slam shut again.

"What was that?" Amanda asked.

"You city kids up yet?" Drew asked, as he popped his head around the corner.

"We just woke up." Todd answered.

Drew shook his head. "Unbelievable. Me and the hands have already had breakfast and done a couple hours work."

"I don't know why we're so sleepy this morning," Todd said with a yawn.

"My dad said it's because of your trip."

"I think we'll get used to things here pretty soon."

"I hope so. Anyway, you're supposed to come on up to the house and have breakfast. My dad's out checking some fences with his old jeep, so I'm going to give you a tour of the ranch buildings as soon as you eat."

"That sounds exciting," Amanda squealed.

"It ain't too exciting if you live here. Hurry up. We'll be waiting." With that he turned and hurried back outside.

"He doesn't seem to like us," Amanda said.

"Could be. But I think it's something else."

"Like what?"

"Well, since he doesn't have any brothers and sisters, and he lives way out here, I don't think he has any friends except wherever his school is. Then we came along and his parents start to make a big fuss over us. He might not like that."

"I know. Why don't we ask his mother if he can stay in the bunkhouse with us on the nights we're here?"

"That's a great idea. I'll ask this morning." He ran back to his room and threw on a shirt and jeans. When he came back into his sister's room with his shoes and socks, she was standing over her suitcase with one hand on her hip and one finger tapping her chin.

"Now let me see. What should I wear this morning? The pink outfit or the green? The yellow one just looks so cute."

"We're on a ranch in the middle of nowhere. I hardly think cute is going to work."

"Then what do you think?"

"I think you didn't bring along enough jeans."

"You're impossible. You know it?"

"You heard Drew. We're going to be crawling around in all those buildings. You should put on the crummiest thing you brought."

"Yeah. *You* sure did," she sneered as she stared at Todd.

"Whatever you do, do it fast. We gotta go eat. I'll be in the living room."

Amanda soon came bounding out to join him. She was wearing jeans and a T-shirt.

"That's more like it," her brother complimented.

Then they were off to the big house. To get there they had to walk on a long gravel path with big logs on each side. The stones made a funny crunching sound with each step they took.

"Don't you think this place is great, Todd?"

"Sure do. I could move out here tomorrow."

"Uncle Reid keeps everything so nice and clean."

They came to the house which had a porch running the

full length in front. The boards were painted in a shiny gray color that matched the trim around the doors and windows. The rest of the house was white with a black roof. All the windows had large gray shutters. On the porch Todd noticed a wooden swing hooked to the ceiling. It was big enough for three people to sit in. There were rocking chairs all over the place with big pillows and a mat in front of the door with the words "Howdy Pardner" printed in bright red. Todd knocked on the door.

"Make sure to wipe your feet, Mandy."

"Come in, come in. Welcome. How did you sleep?" their aunt asked.

"Like a dog in front of the fireplace after a big dinner," Todd told her. Then he stretched his arms.

"Listen, you don't have to knock when you come up here. Our home is your home. You just come on in whenever you want."

Just then Todd's stomach growled, real loud.

"Is your tummy happy or sad?" she asked.

"I think it's happy because my nose just told it about all the good things I'm about to send down there."

"We try to eat a big breakfast on the ranch because the work is hard, and the days can be long."

The children sat at the table and ate like a couple of grunting farm pigs, without the grunting. When they finished, Todd let out a huge belch. He quickly covered his mouth and said, "Excuse me."

"Todd!" his sister scolded.

"Really, I didn't mean to. It just kinda slipped out by

itself."

"That's all right, Todd. It is said in some countries that burping after a good meal is a compliment to the cook."

"We don't do that at our house," Amanda proudly informed her.

"We really don't do it here either, dear."

"Could we be excused please?" Todd asked.

"Certainly. Drew asked that I tell you two to meet him in the barn when you finish here. He's ready to take you on a tour."

"Could I ask you a question first?" Todd asked.

"What is it?"

"Mandy and I were wondering if Drew could sleep out in the bunkhouse with us while we're here."

"That would be nice. Don't tell him I told you, but he was really hoping you'd ask him to do that."

"Great! Let's go," Todd exclaimed. The children dashed to the back door and ran out to the barn. When they got there, they found their cousin at the top of a stack of hay bales as high as a three-story building.

"Whatcha doin' up there, Drew?" Amanda asked.

"I'm stacking this stuff so we can feed some of our animals next winter."

"Does it snow out here?"

"Does it snow?" he repeated to her. "Does it snow?" Then he started laughing. He laughed so hard it made him fall down on the stack of hay where he started rolling around like an old hound dog.

"When it snows in Wyoming, we can't can't go outside for days sometimes. If we do, we have to string a rope between the buildings or a guy could get lost and die out in the cold."

"Really?" Todd challenged.

"Really. The snow can get so high it covers the first level of our whole house."

"That much?"

He got back to his feet, and then jumped right off the hay and into the air. It made Amanda scream, but he grabbed a rope that was hanging nearby and slid down like a fireman.

"Hey, Drew," Todd said. "We were wondering something."

"What's that?" he asked as he headed toward the large open doors of the barn.

"Would you like to stay out with us in the bunkhouse while we're here?"

"That old place? Why would a guy want to stay out there? I could do that any night of the week, any week of the year, any old time."

Todd turned and winked at his sister. "Well, it's up to you. We just thought it might be fun."

"Tell you what, kids. I'll think about it. Okay?"

"What ever you say, Drew. Out here, you're the boss."

Drew stopped right in his tracks, spun around, and studied Todd and his sister for a few seconds. "You know what? You guys are all right. Sure, I'd like to. So, do you want to see the rest of the place or not?"

Todd noticed someone moving at the far end of the hay

bales. He wore a black shirt, black jeans, and a black hat. It looked to Todd like this guy was in a hurry. No sooner had he seen him than he quickly disappeared through a far door.

"Who was that?" he asked.

"That? That's Travis. He works for us."

"Oh, right. He was on the radio last night when your dad called him after we almost smashed into a big bull in the middle of the road."

"And when we just about ran into a truck with its lights off," his sister added.

"I was there. Remember?"

Todd continued. "Well, your dad told us it might be rustlers. He called Travis to call the sheriff and report it."

"Travis . . . calling the sheriff . . . about rustlers? Now that's a good one." He took one look at his cousins and added, "Never mind."

"Let's go," Todd said.

For the next two hours they explored every building and storage shed on the ranch. There was only one place left that they hadn't seen. Todd especially wondered what it was used for because it was very tall with equally towering double sliding steel doors across the entire front. On top he saw an orange thing that looked like a pennant, only it was wide and round at the front, about six feet long, and tapering to a hole at the end.

"What's that thing?" he asked

"It's a wind sock."

"A wind sock?" Amanda asked. "What's the wind need

socks for?"

"It isn't for the wind. Well, it kinda is. It shows a pilot what direction the wind is blowing so he can tell which way to take off or land."

"Planes fly out here?"

"C'mon, I'll show you." Drew walked up to a metal post. It had a black box attached to it. He opened the the small lid to the box where Todd could see a keypad with numbers and letters. His cousin punched in a code and then the most amazing thing happened. First, he heard a loud bell, like when a class was finished at school. Then, slowly, and with a low rumble, the two massive doors began to move in opposite directions.

"Wow! I've never seen anything like that!"

The doors continued to open slowly as Amanda hid behind her brother. Then she peeked out just in time to see a silver propeller and the nose of a yellow and orange airplane.

"Whose is that?" Todd asked.

"It's my dad's."

"Is not."

"Is too!" No sooner had Drew said that than they heard the sound of a car coming up behind them. Todd turned to look as an old jeep came sliding to a stop in a cloud of dust so thick he couldn't see anything for almost a whole minute.

"Good morning," a cheerful voice said from inside the cloud. "Are you enjoying your tour so far?"

"Uncle Reid?"

"None other. How you kids doing? Is my son treating you

okay?"

"Yeah, he's great."

"I'm going to stay with them in the bunkhouse starting tonight."

"That sounds like a great idea. Now, tell you what. I have another great . . . even greater idea."

"You do?" Todd asked.

"How'd you kids like to see the rest of the ranch?"

"Yes!" they screamed together as they scrambled to climb up into the jeep.

"No, no, no, not in this old thing. I mean up in the air."

"Who knows how to fly?"

"Well, I do, and I've been teaching Drew, too."

"You know how to fly, Drew?"

"Sure I do, once we get up there, but I can't land . . . not yet."

"So what are we waiting for?" their uncle asked.

"I just have one question," Amanda said. "If you have your own airplane, how come you had to drive to the airport to get us?"

"That was unfortunate. We had planned to fly down to get you, but my compass went out two days before you came. Then, about the time we started driving back here from the airport, my plane was being fixed. Today is the first time I've taken it up since the broken part got replaced."

The children jumped out of the jeep and walked toward the plane while their uncle moved the jeep under a big shade tree. Then he joined them in the hanger.

"Go ahead and let them in, Drew. I need to do a little preflight."

Drew seemed very familiar with his dad's plane. He knew how to open the door, how the seats worked, and everything. In no time, he had his cousins buckled up in the two middle seats. Then he plopped down in the copilot's seat just as his dad stepped up on the wing, came through the door, and sat behind the controls.

Todd had never been up in a small airplane like this before, and he was extremely excited. When the powerful engines turned over and the propellers began spinning, the whole plane vibrated. He reached over, took hold of his sister's hand, and squeezed it. His uncle pushed a couple levers, the engines roared louder, and the plane started slowly rolling out into the sunshine.

Right then Todd decided he could get used to living on a ranch like this. *It seems like something exciting happens here every day and night,* he thought.

Chapter 7

Uncle Reid's plane rolled down a bumpy little road with two ruts in it just the size of the skinny wheels underneath. When they came to a wide grassy area, Todd's uncle moved the plane into the center of that strip, checked some dials in front of him, and put his foot on the brake. Then he took a minute to look up into the sky and out both sides of the plane. Todd couldn't exactly figure out what he was looking for because there sure weren't any other airplanes for as far as he could see.

The engines roared even louder than before. Todd felt the plane struggling to get moving, but the brakes held it back like the leash on old Stony at the park back in the city.

I miss Stony, he thought.

Then Uncle Reid took his foot off the brake, and they started rolling forward. At first they moved slowly down the runway, then faster and faster until Todd noticed a queasy feeling in his stomach like the time his dad took him on a roller coaster. He looked out to see a shadow of the plane getting smaller and smaller on the ground below.

"Hey, Todd, didn't you say you wanted to see Devil's Tower?"

"Yes. Could we?"

"I'll take you over there first."

The plane soon leveled off as the sun burst in through the windows. Todd couldn't remember the sky ever looking this blue back home. His uncle had a microphone and headset on. He began talking to someone Todd couldn't see, using words he didn't know, and a lot of numbers and letters. Todd figured it must be some kind of pilot talk or something.

"Okay, kids. Devil's Tower dead ahead."

Todd strained to spot it, but all he saw were trees, tall grass, and a lot of rocks and dirt. "Where?"

"Out there," his uncle pointed.

Todd squinted again, and there, way off in the distance, he thought he did see something. "You mean that little speck way out there?"

"Good eye. That's it all right."

"But it's smaller than I thought."

His uncle laughed. "That's because it's still a few miles away, and we're up in the air. Don't worry, it'll get bigger. I promise."

In just a few minutes Devil's Tower began to look like a giant clay model sticking right out of the ground. The mountain had a flat round top, but it was the sides that were the most interesting. They looked as if enormous grizzly bears had used them for a scratching post. There were straight lines cut right into the tall vertical sides, all the way around, and they stretched from the very top all the way to the very bottom.

"It's huge!" Amanda exclaimed.

Uncle Reid began to make a wide, slow turn until they flew around the rock tower in a perfect circle. Todd counted and they circled three times.

"It looks exactly like the model my friend made in geography class. Only this one is much better."

"The real thing usually is better. Okay, Drew. Wanna take over for me?"

Drew held the control tightly with both hands. Todd noticed that his knuckles started turning white and little beads of sweat began forming on his cousin's upper lip. His eyes were locked straight out the front window, and he hardly blinked.

"Remember, son. Relax. Make sure you keep the little plane in this control . . . here . . . level." The plane was now heading away from Devil's Tower and back toward the ranch. Todd thought Drew was doing a pretty good job.

"That's fine, Son. Do you want to let your cousins have a turn?"

"Sure."

"Todd first!" Amanda yelled.

"Okay, you're up."

Drew squeezed between the front seats and made room for Todd to come up. After they had changed seats, it was Todd's turn to have white knuckles and sweat on his lip, plus everywhere else.

"This is fun. I didn't know it could be so easy. Mandy, wanna try?"

Then a gust of cross wind made the nose dip slightly so that Todd's uncle had to grab the control.

"No, thank you. That's all right," she said.

"You sure?"

"Positive!"

Todd flew for about ten minutes. His uncle only had to make a couple of minor adjustments. Then he said, "Okay, I'll take over from here."

Todd slithered into the back seat again as his cousin moved up to the front. The plane dropped lower in the sky until it looked like it wasn't flying much higher than a tall tree. Todd quickly looked out all the windows to make sure none of those were nearby. His uncle flew past other rock formations, through canyons, over rivers, and rugged hills.

"Where are the animals?" Todd asked.

"Most of them should be over this way." With that, the plane made a steep turn and headed right into the sun. Todd had to cover his eyes for a minute until the plane turned again.

"There they are . . . some of them at least," Uncle Reid announced.

As Todd looked out, he could see hundreds of reddish-colored animals with white patches on some parts of their bodies. "Are those all yours?"

"Sure are . . . those and a whole lot more. This week we'll pack up a bunch of horses with food and gear, and then head out for our spring roundup."

"I can't wait," Todd said.

Amanda looked over at him. "I can," she groaned.

"Hey, wait a minute. What was that?" their uncle asked in an alarmed tone.

"What was what?" Drew asked.

"I'm not sure. I'll take her in for a better look." They made another sharp turn, steeper than before. Todd had to look straight up in order to see his sister who was now sitting above his head. The plane leveled off again, then dropped down until Todd thought his feet could touch the ground if he put them out there. They went speeding along a barbed wire fence for several hundred feet. Then Uncle Reid yelled, "There, that!" Again the plane soared into the sky and made a steep turn in the opposite direction. This time Todd was looking straight down at his sister. And his stomach wasn't feeling too well either.

"I'm sorry for the rough ride, kids. Is everyone okay?"

"Not me," Todd said in a quivering voice.

"Well, it's my fault. Sorry. If you're feeling a little woozy, there's a bag in the seat pocket in front of you. Feel free to deposit your breakfast in there if you need to."

It was a good thing he said that, or everyone in the plane would have been wearing Todd's breakfast. He grabbed a bag and ripped it open just in time to say goodbye to all those good things his aunt had cooked for him.

"We call that giving it the old heave ho," Drew joked. "Don't worry. It's happened to me, too. But you get used to flying after a few times. Now you're a member of the Wyatt *Urp* Club."

Todd turned to his sister and noticed she looked all chalky white. She was staring straight ahead, didn't blink, and didn't say a word. He quickly grabbed another bag just in time to put it over her mouth. She made what he did look like a warm- up act for the main event. It took her two bags before she was done.

"If we go up again, I think we should eat a smaller breakfast. Then we'll have less to hurl," Todd told her with a twitching smile.

Uncle Reid was intent on studying the landscape. "Look there, Drew. You see it?"

"Yeah, the fence is busted."

"Cut is more like it. Do you see those tire tracks?"

"Oh, yeah, I do. Rustlers you think?"

"Rustlers I know."

Uncle Reid flipped a switch on his radio and called out, "Base, this is Reid Rider. Over."

"Read you Reid Rider. What's up?"

"That you, Travis?"

"Yes, sir."

"I don't know what it is, but whenever you have radio watch, we seem to call in repeated rustler reports."

"I know. Got another one?"

"I think so. We're off in the north fork area, and one of the fences has definitely been split wide open. I see two sets of big tire tracks and three or four sets of smaller ones."

"Want me to report it to the sheriff?"

"Affirmative. Get your map out and give him the coordinates."

"Will do. Out."

"I'd like to give you a longer tour, kids, but we need to get to the ranch." With that, the plane turned again, but not as steeply as before, and headed back. Uncle Reid had a serious look on his face. Todd could tell that something was very wrong.

In about fifteen minutes, the ranch came into view just ahead. The plane made one wide circle around the buildings and lined up with the grassy runway straight ahead of them. The wheels touched the ground, bounced into the air, and touched again. They taxied up in front of the hanger. Todd's uncle gunned the motors, and the plane turned around in a small circle. Then he switched off both engines, and the propellers slowed to a stop. There was still a spinning sound in the front of the plane, but that also soon stopped.

"Okay. Everybody out."

Drew turned and looked back to Todd. The look on his face said he wanted to tell him something, but he couldn't. Not just now. Todd wondered why he suddenly seemed so serious. He remembered what Drew had said about Travis. *Could he be helping the Rustlers?* Todd wondered. *Couldn't be,* he thought. *He works for my uncle.*

Chapter 8

Drew, Todd, and a couple of the ranch hands helped push the airplane back into its hanger.

"Make sure to gas her up," Uncle Reid said. "No telling when I may need to go up again, especially now."

That really gave Todd a nervous feeling. *Wonder what could be happening?* he thought.

Drew motioned for Todd and his sister to follow him. They walked around the corner of one of the buildings where no one could see them. Todd decided this was his chance to ask some questions.

"Hey, Drew, hold up." His cousin went over to a fence, sat down, and leaned against the rough wooden post. He picked up a piece of tall grass that had a green pod on the top.

"Watch," he told them, "I call these things torpedo plants."

"Is that their real name?" Amanda asked.

"They're just weeds. It's what I do with them that makes the torpedo." He looped the bottom end of the stalk around the upper end just below the pod.

"Now watch this." With a quick motion he forced the loop up into the bottom of the pod, which caused it to break off from the stalk. It flew clear across the lane from where they were sitting and bounced off the side of the building.

Todd looked on in amazement. "Can I try that?"

"Sure. There's no shortage of them on this ranch."

For the next several minutes all three children picked the weeds and fired pods at the building, at each other, and straight up in the air to see how far they would go. Amanda even got pretty good at it.

"Hey," Drew said, "let's have a contest to see how far we can shoot 'em."

They all tried, but it was impossible to decide whose pod was whose. It was kind of like trying to find a green golf ball, in the grass, in the dark, at night.

They were ready for a change and before Drew could offer a suggestion, Todd said, "So Drew, tell me more about Travis."

"What do you mean?"

"You know."

"I do?"

"Yeah. Somethin' doesn't seem right about that guy, and you know it."

"Promise not to tell anyone if I tell you?"

"Sure, I promise."

"I don't," Amanda protested.

"Then you don't have to stick around and listen," Todd scolded.

"Oh, all right. I'll stay. Wouldn't want to miss anything good."

"Then you promise, too?"

"I guess so."

"Well, this is what I know."

Just then they heard, "Drew, where are you? Drew!"

"It's Travis. You guys stay here. I'll be right back." Drew ran around the corner and was only gone about two minutes. Todd and his sister waited, wondering what dark secret he was about to tell them. Drew came sprinting back around the corner and reported, "After lunch we're going to teach you to ride your horses and how to do some rope tricks."

"Do we have to?" Amanda complained.

"Not unless you don't want to become a real rootin', tootin' cowboy."

"Ish, no. I never want to be a cowboy," she said with a frown.

"Same goes for cowgirls."

"I just can't win."

"But Drew, you were about to tell us some news."

"I was?"

"About Travis."

"That's right, I was. Now I only know this from what my dad has told me and from some of the talk I've heard around the ranch."

"So, what is it?" Todd asked.

"Yeah, tell us will ya?"

"It seems ol' Travis there used to be a lowlife cattle rustling scum."

"No kidding?"

"No kidding. And that's not the worst part of it. He got caught stealing cattle from this very ranch."

"Whew," Todd said with a whistle. "But now he works for your dad. How come?"

"My dad looks pretty tough, and he acts tough, too. Shoot, he is tough, but he has a real soft heart when it comes to people. I've seen him bring some of the most washed up, dried out, crusty old men to this place. He cleans them up, gives them a place to stay, makes sure they have food to eat, and if they can, he lets them stay on and work some."

"That is so sweet," Amanda cooed.

"You might think so, but I think it makes things too easy for some really shifty characters to get on this ranch. A lot of those old guys have died out here."

"Then what?"

"My dad tries to find out where they come from, but most don't have any family at all. So he has someone from town come out to get them, and they get buried in part of the cemetery in a spot my dad owns."

"Why does he do that?"

"Search me? Except he keeps telling me that, in this world, sometimes you have to act like Jesus with skin on. That's probably the only Jesus some of these people will ever see."

"So what's the deal with Travis? He isn't old, or dried

out, or crispy. He's young."

"He's a special case. My dad found out that Travis had a dad that got drunk and beat him up a lot. Travis tried to tell the judge that's the reason he turned out bad. But if there's one thing my dad really hates, its somebody who tries to blame other people for their mistakes or for the bad things they do."

"Why should *he* care?"

"He thinks we'd have a better country if people tried to do right."

"And Travis?"

"Travis was supposed to go up the river to the big house for at least five years."

"What?" Amanda asked.

"Prison." Then Todd added, "Instead he's here, working. So what happened?"

"The judge is a friend of my dad's. They worked it out so Travis could come to live out here and work for a couple of years. If he can prove that he's honest and won't steal anymore, then the judge will let him go."

"How scary," Amanda whispered.

"That's what I think. So I try to stay away from him unless other people are around. The truth is, I just don't trust the guy."

"Drew, where are you?" a voice called again from around the building.

"It's that Travis again. Isn't it?" Todd whispered fearfully.

"Afraid so. Let's go see what the thief wants." As they walked around the corner, not only did they see Travis, they also found six other cowboys riding in slowly on their horses. Each one wore a broad cowboy hat, jeans, leather coverings over their legs, and tall cowboy boots. They looked pretty dusty to Todd, and the horses were all sweaty.

"Come over here, kids, I want to show you something," Travis called.

Todd was a little nervous now just thinking about being near somebody who should really be in prison, but he went over anyway. As he walked nearer, he noticed that each cowboy also held a big white plastic bucket in one hand.

"How'd you boys do?" Travis asked.

"Got sixteen of 'em this morning."

"Not bad. How far did you have to go out?"

"Not far at all. Seems they're comin' in closer every year."

"They must be getting a little too used to people," Travis noted.

"What are you guys talking about?" Todd asked. "Who's coming closer and getting too used to people?"

"Snakes."

"Snakes!" Amanda shrieked, "I really hate those things."

"What kind are they?" Todd asked.

"Rattlesnakes." Just the name made Amanda shudder.

"You don't really have to be afraid of them," Travis said.

"Why would you say something like that?" Todd asked. "Rattlesnakes are one of the most deadly snakes we have."

"That's true, but that's not the whole story."

"It's the only part of the story I care to know about,"

Amanda complained.

"They've been called the gentlemen of all snakes."

"Humph," Todd snorted. "I'll bet if I went around sinking my teeth into people nobody'd call me a gentleman."

"But they don't do that."

"You got a different kind of rattler out here?"

"Same kind. The thing is rattlesnakes will only bite if they feel threatened. But, before they do that, they give out a warning. You can hear them from a ways off just shaking that tail like a baby's rattle. It's like they're saying, 'Here I am, waaay over here, in this tall grass, next to the big rock. Better not come over here because I might bite you.'

"Then if you come closer, he starts right back in saying, 'I told you, I'm right here. Can't you hear my rattle? What's the matter with you? Now go away!' The rattler says, 'I'm warning you one more time.' Then if a guy is too stupid to leave him alone, well, wham!" That made Amanda shudder again.

"Then how did you guys get so close without being bit?"

One of the cowboys pulled a pole out of the side of his saddle. It had a big loop at the end, and he began pulling on the pole as it extended longer and longer. "We use one of these snares. If the snake bites it, he's just going to get a toothache."

"Anyway, every few weeks we go on a rattlesnake roundup."

"How does it work?" Todd asked.

"We just ride around and listen. When we hear one saying, 'Yoo hoo, over here,' we get off our horse, walk up, put the snare around his head, lift him up, and drop him in the bucket."

"Do you kill them?" Amanda questioned.

"Now why would we want to do that?" asked one of the men.

"They're rattlesnakes aren't they? What more reason would you need?" she replied.

"We're only interested in keeping this part of the ranch cleared of those critters to keep the people and animals safe. The ones that live farther out we just leave alone."

"Well, what do you do with the ones you catch?" Amanda asked. "I don't want to go anywhere near that place!"

"Sometimes we'll ride out about a mile from where we found it, and just drop him off."

"Why?" Todd wanted to know.

"You aren't supposed to take rattlers very far away. It isn't good for them."

Todd noticed something as the cowboys walked their horses over to a pickup truck parked in one of the storage buildings. It had a big box in the back. Very carefully they walked up, one by one, opened the top to their bucket, and eased the snakes into the box.

"We're going to take this bunch on over to the Wildlife Research Program. They study them there."

"What's to study?"

"Lots of things."

"Like for instance?"

"Let me see. Did you know the babies are born alive just

like you and me?"

"They are?"

"Uh huh. Every couple years they have about ten babies."

"The grown-ups shed their skin about four times a year," another cowboy added.

"What do they do with it?"

"Nothing. It just gets left behind. Each time the skin falls off they get a new rattle ring on their tail."

"Cool," Todd said. "So can you tell how old they are by the number of rattles, like the rings in a tree?"

"It isn't the best way to tell because rattlesnakes live a pretty rough life out there. Lots of times some of the rattles fall off."

"What else do the snakes do?"

"They sleep all winter."

"Like bears?"

"Exactly like bears."

"All I want to know is how big do they get?" Amanda asked in a trembling voice.

"They can get up to seven feet long, but most of them are only three to four feet. I expect ours will be about that size. Do you want to see them?"

"No!" Amanda said as her brother moved closer toward the truck.

"Do people really die if they get bitten?" he asked.

"Some do. It depends on how close the bite is to the heart, how old the person is, and things like that. Actually, more people die from bee stings than from rattlesnake bites."

"What do you do if one bites you?"

"Have you met Cookie yet?"

"Cookie? Who's Cookie?"

"He runs the chuck wagon on the cattle roundups."

"No, we don't know him."

"Well, he carries an antidote for different kinds of bites and stuff. If a snake were to bite you, Cookie could give you a shot in just a few seconds to fight the poison. Then they still would have to get you to a hospital as fast as they could. A rattlesnake bite is a very serious thing. Luckily, like I said, it doesn't happen all that often."

"Have you ever been bitten, Travis?"

"No, but I came pretty close a couple of times."

"Didn't you hear the rattle?" Amanda asked.

"Let's just say I was in kind of a hurry when it happened, but no, I've never been bitten. And I never want to be."

"A couple of the hands have," Drew told them, "but they're okay now."

"Anyway," Travis continued, "these little guys are going to the research place. They milk the venom."

"Yuck. What for?" Amanda grunted.

"Some of the scientists think they might find a cure for cancer from studying the effects of the venom or something. I'm not exactly sure. I've just heard about it. Come on, I'll show you the snakes."

As Todd neared the truck, he could hear the sound of

several rattles. Just that scary warning made him shiver. He imagined himself out in the middle of a canyon someplace, all alone. His horse had fallen and died, so he had to walk out. Then, suddenly, he tripped and fell into a deep hole. When his eyes adjusted to the dim light, he began to sense that there were sticks scattered all over the floor of the pit. Then, in his mind, he could see the sticks start to move. Not only did they move, but they began to rattle, first one, then another, and another, until the entire pit made the sound of a rushing river over huge boulders. The thought of that made Todd shake all over. Still, he went closer to the truck so he could have a look. Amanda stayed back.

The box in the truck had a metal top, but the sides were made of a strong, clear plastic. Like peering into a horrifying dream, Todd looked on in amazement at the sight of so many snakes all in one place. He came around the tailgate of the truck for a better look. Then he climbed in and inched his way right up to the back of the box. When he did that, one of the biggest snakes, all coiled up inside, suddenly lunged out toward Todd, striking the inside of the plastic barrier with its nose. He hit so hard it made a loud sound like a ninety-five mile-an-hour fastball as it smacks into the catcher's mitt at a big- league baseball game.

The snake's strike stunned Todd so badly he just froze right where he was. Then, without warning, he jumped up like a jack-in-the-box and didn't stop until he was three feet away from the back of the truck. He thought it must have looked really funny because everyone laughed, but he wasn't laughing. He had never been that frightened at any time in all his life. The thought of having only a thin clear barrier between himself and those razor-sharp fangs left him shaken.

Todd's mind was fixed on that snake, and he stood so still it almost seemed like he was hypnotized. *Man,* he thought, *I don't ever want to come that close to another snake again as long as I live.*

"You kids go get some lunch," Travis instructed. "We'll work on the horses and ropes when you come back."

As the children walked back toward the big house, Todd didn't make a sound.

Chapter 9

Aunt Debbie reminded Todd of his own mom because she was always cheerful. Boy, could she ever cook! He was happy to take a lunch break just to see what she would come up with next. Today was "build your own tacos" day. The children sat around the table talking, eating, and laughing.

After lunch, Amanda asked, "Can I go out and play with the kitties?" The ranch had dozens of them.

"Most are a little wild, honey," Aunt Debbie cautioned, "but I'll give you some scraps that you can put in a dish. The ones that come up to eat are a little more friendly than the others. Just be careful."

"I will." She scampered out the side door with a metal plate of food calling, "Here you cutsie, wootsie kitties." Todd went along with her. They sat on the side steps as six smaller kittens ventured in to smell the food. Then three of those came in close enough to eat. The children began to pet them on the heads and scratch their ears. That made the kittens purr.

"Hey Mandy," Todd asked, "what do you think of Travis?"

"I think he's very nice. Why?"

"I still don't trust him, and I plan to keep an eye on him, too."

Drew came out the door with a plate of cookies. "Time for dessert," he told them. Then Travis started calling for them again.

"Doesn't that guy ever quit?" Todd complained.

"If you want to go out on the trail ride, you're going to have to learn how to get on a horse and stay on. C'mon, let's go." The plate was left behind, but the cookies all disappeared.

The children dashed around the side of the house and headed toward the corral where a few horses were standing. Some of the cowboys sat on top of the fence.

"I think they wanted good seats for the show," Drew teased.

"What show?"

"You guys, that's who. You're the main attraction. They're probably already trying to decide how many times you'll fall off."

As they came closer, Todd could see the horses were already saddled up.

"Are these things tame?" he asked.

"Tame?" one of the guys on the fence yelled. "They're not tame. We just brought 'em in from the range this morning. These beasts are totally wild."

Todd felt that same sinking feeling in his stomach. He wasn't sure he really needed to go out on a dumb trail ride after all. But, unfortunately, his sister was the animal lover in the family. Show her an animal, and she'd make friends with it in five minutes . . . guaranteed.

"Who wants to go first?" Travis shouted.

"I will," she replied.

This is just great, Todd thought. *Now I'm going to have a girl show me up.* He was still afraid to see his sister thrown out of her saddle and hit the ground like a sack of horse feed. He really was worried she might get hurt. Travis pulled her through the rails in the fence, and hoisted her up on top of a sleek brown horse with a white face. She sat in the saddle like she was born riding a horse.

"What do I do now?" she asked Travis.

"You take these reins, one in each hand. If you want your horse to go, you just nudge him in the sides with your heels. Want to go left, pull on the left rein. To go right, pull the right. If you want to stop, pull back on both of them and say, "Whoa!"

"That reminds me of your joke about a preacher and a horse," Drew snickered, "but it'll keep till later."

After Travis had her settled on the horse, he climbed onto one of the others and brought it alongside Amanda. "Ready to give it a try?"

"Okay." She gave the horse a nudge with her heels, only she forgot she was still pulling back on the reins. Again she nudged, and again the horse just stood there.

"Loosen up on the reins a little. Then try again."

"Oh, right. I forgot." She did as he had instructed, and the horse began walking forward.

"Okay now, left turn," Travis instructed. Todd couldn't believe his eyes as his sister's horse made a perfect left turn.

"All right," Todd said. "I think I'm ready now." Drew helped him climb up on a jet-black horse. After watching his sister, he felt he was ready to go with nobody helping him. Todd was like that. He nudged his horse but instead of taking a few gentle steps, this beast lunged forward and took off into a full gallop.

"Whoa! Whoa!" Todd screamed as he pulled the reins back as hard as he could. It was no use. The horse was bigger than he was and seemed to have his own plans. He ran up to the fence on the opposite side of the corral. Todd thought his horse planned to jump the thing so he got ready to go flying into the air. He did go flying, but not because of a powerful jump.

His horse went right up to the edge of the fence and then stopped dead still. Since Todd's body was still traveling as fast as a horse at full gallop, he simply sailed into the air. He was still holding the reins, which did him no good since the horse was now behind him. Then he reached the end of the reins. When that happened, Todd snapped back slightly, did a complete summersault in mid-air, and came crashing to the ground on the other side of the fence.

All the cowboys started to hoot, holler, clap, and laugh. "I'll give that boy a ten!" one of them called out.

"More like a ten times ten," laughed another.

Todd felt around to see if anything was broken. There wasn't, except for his pride.

"Sorry, Todd," Travis said as he rode up to the fence. "I must have picked one out for you that was just a little too frisky."

After what Drew had told him, Todd wondered if Travis did that on purpose, but there was no way to prove it. Travis went back over and took the reins of a dark brown horse with a black mane and tail. "Here little buddy, why don't you try this one?"

Who does he think he is, calling me his 'little buddy' anyway? Todd thought angrily. He stood up, brushed the dust from his clothes, and headed back into the corral. He remembered something his dad used to say, "If you fall off a horse, son, the best thing to do is get right back on." That advice had never made any sense to him until now.

"No thanks, I'll try Black Ugly again." He climbed up by himself and began making the horse do what he wanted, not what the horse wanted. After a brief moment, it worked out pretty well.

For over two hours the children practiced with their horses in the safety of the fenced-in corral. Then Travis said, "It's time to take them out for a real ride."

Todd wasn't sure if he was quite ready for that, especially since he thought his horse could run clear to California without stopping if he wanted to. He kept an extra-firm grip on the reins. Travis took them out onto a narrow trail that lead up into the high country.

"I want you to practice in a few places so you'll be comfortable with the trail we take for the roundup," he explained. They continued riding up and down hills, into small gullies, and through thick brush. Then Travis announced, "That's enough for one day. Time to head back in."

Todd was glad to hear that because his backside was starting to feel like someone had been kicking him all the way up and down those hills. Plus, he was hurting from that nasty fall he'd taken earlier. Since most of the trail they were returning on sloped downward, the trip was quicker than going up. Once in the horse barn, everyone dismounted. Some of the other cowboys came up to take off the saddles and give the horses a little feed and water.

"That was fun," Amanda sighed.

"Yeah," Todd added. He turned to Travis, "Didn't you say something about showing us some rope tricks?"

"That's next on the schedule. I'll get the ropes and you kids can meet me at the corral," Travis suggested. A few minutes later he was there with a length of rope for each of them. Drew took his, made a loop, and immediately began swinging it over his head, dropping it to the ground, and jumping in and out of the spinning circle.

"Man, Drew, how did you learn to do that?" Todd asked.

"Practice my friend. Lot and lots of practice."

"Here," Travis offered as he handed a rope to Amanda. Then he gave one to Todd.

"The first thing you have to do is make your lasso. Here, I'll show you." He proceeded to make a loop at one end of the rope and handed it to Todd. Then he did the same thing for

Amanda.

"Now the flat loop is the roper's first trick, and it's the easiest."

"That's good," Todd said, "because I have no idea what I'm doing." Just then, his sister took her rope, swung it around twice and got all tangled from her head to her knees.

"Help, I'm stuck," she complained. Travis came over and unraveled the pile of spaghetti she had managed to make out of her rope.

"Thanks," she sighed.

"Watch me," Travis said. "You let the loop part hang down, and you hold onto the rest of the rope. Then reach down and make it into a square shape with your hands in two corners and your feet in the other two."

"Like this?" Todd asked.

"That looks pretty good. Next, you'll want to spin the loop in the opposite way than a clock goes."

"Watch me," Drew hollered. He began spinning his rope. When he did that, it turned into a perfect circle all by itself.

"What makes it do that?" Todd asked

"You might not understand it," Travis said, "but gravity holds the rope down, and do you know what centrifugal force is?"

"Kind of."

"Because your loop is held in place on one side as you spin it and because you are turning it with the straight part of the rope, it's forced to stay in the shape of a circle." Then Travis started spinning his rope. With grace and ease he raised it high over his head, keeping it in a perfect circle. Then he spun it round and round his body. Next he passed it back and forth down by his feet and jumped into and out of the big loop.

"That's kind of like the way we girls play jump rope at school."

The thought of jumping rope like a girl made Travis laugh, and his feet got all tangled. He re-formed his loop, spun it high over his head again, stepped into the middle of the loop, and began to move the loop up over his head, then down near his waist, then up again. Next he spun the loop right beside his body. Again he put it over his head, twirled it there three or four times, and then cast it out until it fell perfectly over Drew's head.

"Hey, cut that out."

"Here's the next thing I want to show you. The reason for learning the loop first is because all the other rope tricks begin with it. But more important, it's the loop that lets you throw the rope, catch a calf, and bring him down. We'll be doing some of that on the roundup. So practice making the loop for a few minutes, and I'll come back to see how you're doing."

Since Drew was such an expert, he was able to show Amanda and Todd how to make a loop that fit their size. It wasn't long before both of them were at least able to keep their ropes out of the dirt. By that time Travis came back.

He watched them for a few seconds before he commented, "Very, very good. You two are fast learners. Now I want to show you how to throw your rope."

"That's easy," Amanda said, and she coiled all of her rope in one hand, wound her arm around two times, and threw the whole thing over the fence. "See. Nothing to it."

"I didn't mean throw it away. To throw your rope means to cast it out and catch something."

"Oh, sorry," she said sheepishly as she scurried under the fence, grabbed her rope, and got back in place.

"We use that stump over there for practice." Travis twirled his rope over his head two or three times then let it go. Just as he had caught Drew, he made a perfect loop over the stump. The children began to practice that trick. Todd got it on his third try, but Amanda finally had to give up.

"That's okay, Amanda. At least you tried," Travis told her reassuringly.

"It's just that I don't ever see myself trying to rope cattle. I mean, come on."

"That's probably true. I'm sure Cookie will find some other things for you to do once we're in camp."

"I hope so."

"That should do it for now. You'd better get washed up for dinner."

"Exactly when is the roundup?" Todd asked.

"Day after tomorrow."

"Really? I can't wait. Eating camp food, sleeping out under the stars in the big sky country."

"Yeah, with the snakes and other creepy things that live

out there. I'm in no hurry to go," Amanda warned.

"That's up to you, but I think it will be our biggest adventure yet," Todd said with confidence. *And we might be there when they catch some rustlers,* he thought.

Chapter 10

After dinner, Todd and Amanda helped Drew move some of his things into the bunkhouse so he could sleep out there with them. The room he chose was fixed up like an old jail. It had real looking bars with a door and a lock on the bars. His bed was comfortable, and it was decorated with an old-looking army blanket. There was no other furniture behind the bars, but out in the large area of the room sat a big wooden desk. "Wanted" posters covered one entire wall. On the desk sat a sign that said, "Sheriff."

"This is cooler than my mine-shaft room," Todd told him. That seemed to make Drew puff up with pride.

"My dad was a state senator a few years ago. He used to bring some pretty important people out to the ranch for meetings. They always wanted to have their pictures taken in these rooms."

"Drew," Todd began, "I think Travis has been very nice. How come you don't trust him?"

"You've only known him for a few hours. I've lived with

him for almost a year, and I know what I know."

"I still think he's a good guy."

"Think what you like. It won't change anything," Drew grumbled.

Amanda came walking back into the jail room. "Hey, you guys, Drew's mother said we have to get to bed because this has been such a big day."

"Okay, little miss alarm clock, we will," Todd mocked.

"Good night," she said with a yawn and a stretch.

"Sure, whatever," Drew responded. He and Todd talked together for about another hour until they could not keep their eyes open.

"Think I'll head on back to the old mine shaft. See you in the morning."

"Okay, see ya."

Todd could hardly believe it, but the next thing he knew the sun had come up again, and he began to awaken. It wasn't from the sun shining though. He heard something. It sounded like several trucks coming down the dirt lane. He slipped out of his bed, walked to the window, and looked out just as four big white trucks came to a stop. They had police-looking emergency lights on racks across the tops. Painted on each driver's door was a big golden star with the words "Sheriff's Patrol" on it. Men in brown police uniforms got out, and Todd saw his uncle come from the house.

Man, oh man, I wish I knew what they were talking about, he thought. Quickly, he pulled on his jeans and a shirt, and put his shoes on. He didn't even take the time to find his socks. He slipped out the back door of the bunkhouse where several high bushes helped hide him from the police. Slowly, he made his way closer.

"We're making our rounds today to warn all the ranchers in the area," one of the policemen said.

"Warn us about what?"

"Remember the call you made to our office about the bull in the middle of the road, the trailer and truck with no lights, and then the broken fence you saw from the air?"

"Uh huh."

"We've had reports from all over that rustlers are active in this region."

"I thought so," Todd's uncle said. "What do you want us to do?"

"Just be on the lookout. Be alert, and if you see anything suspicious, let us know right away."

"I will. By the way, you might like to know we're planning on a roundup tomorrow."

"That's perfect," the sheriff told him. "We're borrowing a chopper from the state police. Make sure to take your satellite phone along. If you see anything, anything at all, give us a call."

"I'll have it with me, and we'll keep our eyes peeled."

I'd like to catch just one rustler, Todd thought. He crept quietly back toward the door. He was almost there when he caught his arm on a thorn. He nearly let out a scream, but then he remembered he didn't want the men to know he'd been listening. He slapped his hand over his mouth and hurried inside the bunkhouse. Once inside he let out the loudest yell, "Boy that hurt!"

It was so loud that Drew came running from his room and Amanda shuffled out into the hallway from hers. "What's happening?" she asked.

"You guys aren't going to believe it."

"Believe what?" Drew demanded.

"Rustlers. That's what."

"What are you talking about?"

"The sheriff and a bunch of his deputies just came out here. They were talking with your dad so I snuck out to see if I could hear anything."

"And?"

"And I heard plenty."

"Well, what is it?" his sister demanded.

"They warned Uncle Reid that rustlers are working around here someplace and to take his satellite phone and to be on the lookout."

"That's nothin'," Drew sneered. "They warn ranchers like that all the time."

"Yes, but they talked about the bull we saw in the road, the trailer, the broken fence and everything."

"It's still no big deal. Anyway, after breakfast we can go on a practice ride by ourselves. I want to show you some stuff."

"What kind of stuff?"

"You'll see."

The children ate their breakfast a little more quickly than usual so they could get out on the trail as soon as possible. Drew had called out to the barn so one of the hands already had three horses saddled and ready for them.

"Pick your beast," he teased.

Todd and Amanda chose the same horses they had used when they first took their lessons. For some reason the black horse seemed more gentle to Todd today. They climbed up into their saddles and pulled on one rein. The horses each turned toward the door, and they were on their way.

"What did you want to show us?" Todd asked.

"Out here we have a bunch of abandoned mines, broken down ranches, and ghost towns."

Amanda pulled the reins of her horse and said, "Whoa! Nobody told me about any ghosts."

"Not real ghosts, silly. They just call them ghost towns because no one lives there. There aren't really any buildings either, but the old mines are still around."

"Can we see one?" Todd asked.

"We might, but first I want to show you an old ranch house where nobody lives anymore." The children rode on for at least another thirty minutes until they came around the side of a big hill. "There it is," Drew announced.

Just in front of them sat an old house. The paint had long since faded in the sun and the house just seemed to slump to the ground. There were gaping holes in the roof and none of the windows had glass in them. A rusting pickup truck sat in the front yard. Tall weeds grew all around it. The truck had no wheels, the engine was gone, and several other parts were missing.

They dismounted and walked to the old truck. Todd leaned in and noticed the knob was still on the old gearshift.

"Can I have this thing?" he asked.

"Doesn't belong to me. If you can get it off, it's yours."

Todd gripped the knob with one hand and gave it a twist. To his surprise it began turning easily until it came off the top of the gearshift lever. He took it out of the truck and put it in his pocket.

They started walking their horses toward the long-abandoned house, but something caught Todd's eye on the way.

"Hey, Drew. Look at these rocks. This one looks like the rings of an old tree."

"That's because it *is* an old tree."

"But it's a rock."

"Ever hear of petrified wood?"

"Yes. It's wood that is so old it's turned into solid rock, I think."

Todd picked up a couple of pieces and put them in his pocket, too. "I can use some of this stuff to show at school when we get back," he said.

"Whatever," Drew responded.

Todd thought it looked kind of eerie to see old torn curtains inside the house just blowing in the wind. The whole place looked like a painting to him or the page from a picture calendar.

"Isn't it sad?" his sister commented.

"What?"

"That a family used to live here. They probably had kids just like us, and kitties, and a dog I'll bet."

Todd thought for a moment, "Now they're gone, and just this shell is left."

The children walked their horses closer and Drew asked, "Wanna go inside?"

"We *sure* do," Todd responded. All three tied their reins to tree branches so their horses couldn't run away and then headed for the house. As they walked up the stairs, one of the steps crumbled under their weight.

"Be careful," Drew warned. "You could fall right through the floor of this dump."

Once inside, Todd began to imagine how it used to look with people living here . . . rugs on the floor . . . furniture. Some of the wallpaper was still up, but most of it had water stains from years of rain coming through the holes in the roof. They continued to explore, turning over the pots, pans, and jars they found.

"Hey, come over here," Drew called. Todd and his sister joined him. "This is odd." He pointed to a newspaper on the floor, bent down, and picked it up.

"Look at the date. This is from only a week ago."

One of those shivers went right up Todd's back at the thought of someone having been there so recently before him.

"Do you think it was rustlers?"

"Probably just one of those losers my dad keeps trying to help I guess."

Then something terrible happened. There was a thumping sound right above their heads.

"What was that?" Todd asked in a shaky voice.

"I dunno," Drew answered. Slowly, all three heads turned toward the ceiling until six little eyeballs were staring straight up. Then there was another loud thump. It was so hard that part of the ceiling fell in, crashing right beside them. Another louder crash came from outside. Todd and Drew ran to the window just in time to see someone, dressed in black, running into the thick bushes.

Todd wanted to be brave, but he was shaking like the rattles on one of those snakes he saw in the back of the truck. "Was that who I think it was?" he asked.

"Who did you think you saw?" Drew asked.

"Travis."

"Me, too. Let's look upstairs."

"I'm not going up there," Amanda groaned.

"Well, we are!"

Cautiously the boys began climbing the stairs.

"You guys aren't leaving me down here, are you?" Amanda said as she hurried to join them.

"Watch where you step," Drew warned. When they reached the top they could see some things stacked in a room at the end of the hall.

"Let's check that stuff out," Todd suggested. Slowly, they continued down the hall until they entered the broken-down room. Next to the wall was a chest with a lock on it.

"We should break it open," Todd said.

"Not so fast," Drew ordered. "Maybe whoever it belongs to won't know we found it if we just leave it alone."

"That's a good idea. I just wish I knew what was inside. Look over there. Are those letters?" Todd walked over and picked one up. Most of the address part had been torn off, but there was no mistake. He could clearly see the name, Travis.

Chapter 11

The children hurried back to their horses and headed for the ranch. They decided not to tell anyone about what they had seen. Not just yet anyway. Besides, they weren't positive it was Travis, but that envelope with his name on it was too much of a coincidence. Drew led them in a different direction from the way they had first come to the abandoned ranch. Once they came down off the narrow trail from the hills, it led out onto a wide flat area.

"I think my horse likes this way better," Amanda reported. "He's tired of going up and down, up and down all the hills around this place. Aren't you boy?"

"Girl, Mandy. Your horse is a girl."

"Oh. Aren't you happier, girl?"

The children rode silently for the next mile or so until they came to a clump of trees. "I think we'd better ride around these," Drew suggested. "No telling what might be in there."

"Yeah, I think I've had just about enough excitement to last me for the rest of the year," Todd exclaimed. "Besides, the roundup starts tomorrow."

As they came around the other side of the trees and headed in the direction of the ranch, Drew saw something. He put his horse into a full gallop until he was about three hundred yards ahead of the others. Suddenly, he brought his horse to an abrupt stop, much like the way Todd's horse had stopped when it sent him sailing over the fence. In one smooth, fluid motion, Drew slipped out of his saddle and began crawling along the ground on his hands and knees.

When the others caught up with him, Todd asked, "What is it?"

"Tire tracks. That's what."

"What's the big deal about tire tracks?"

"The big deal? No one from our ranch *ever* drives around out here and certainly not with anything this big."

"How do you know that?"

"I just do. Okay?"

"Sure, okay, but what does it mean?"

"Describe the truck and trailer you saw out on the road on your way from the airport."

"Now, let me think. The trailer was gray with mud all over it."

"No, not the color. Tell me about the wheels and the tires."

"Are you serious? Who was looking at the tires?"

"Think. Do you remember anything about them?"

"I do," Amanda said.

Todd sneered at her. "You mean to tell me you were

looking at the wheels?"

"Yes, I was."

"Why in the world were you doing that?"

"Because I've never seen a pickup truck like that before."

"Like what?" Drew asked.

"Well, it had three tires on each side in the back."

"Anything like this?" Drew asked, pointing to a set of fresh triple tire tread marks in the mud.

"Sure. They could have made those," she suggested.

"And the trailer? Do you remember the trailer?"

"Yes. It had single tires on the side I could see, but there were three of them in a straight line."

"Like this pattern over here?"

Amanda walked over to where Drew was pointing. "It could be."

"Well, it's all starting to make sense. Travis is a known rustler. He's been living around here, planning to do it again. Probably he has his friends all over the place. Then you see the truck and trailer, and who do we find in the old abandoned ranch house? Travis I tell ya. And look at these smaller tracks. These come from an ATV."

"What's an ATV?"

"It means All Terrain Vehicle. I've got one you haven't seen yet. And look around here! There are cow hoof prints and cow pies all over the place."

"Oh, yeah, I hadn't noticed."

"Well, at least start noticing the pies unless you'd like to wear that stuff on your shoes."

"Good idea," Todd answered.

"There's nothing more we can do out here. Let's head back to the ranch and get ready for the roundup."

"What about Travis? What do we do about him?"

"Nothing. We just watch him. That's all."

They mounted their horses and hurried toward the ranch. When they rode into the barn, none of the children said anything about what they had seen. Even at dinner that night they kept their secret.

"Tonight," Uncle Reid began, "you need to get your roughest clothes and shoes together. We'll be leaving at five A.M."

"Without any breakfast?" Amanda complained.

"Don't worry. Cookie will have it packed for us." Uncle Reid smiled at Amanda and with emphasis said, "We have almost a day's ride before we can camp for the night. Several of the ranch hands have taken the chuck wagon and our gear on ahead. They have everything we need for the roundup. Of course, we have to ride our own horses out to our campsite."

"No staying up late tonight, kids," their aunt warned.

"We won't."

After dinner, they headed for the bunkhouse. Drew brought his old clothes with him, but Todd and Amanda had to get theirs out. That didn't take much time, so they decided to go to the living room and make some plans.

Todd began, "Suppose there are rustlers, and suppose Travis is in on it. What can we do?"

"If we can prove it, then my dad will see him for what he is, have him arrested, and thrown in prison where people like him belong. That's what we can do."

"But I still think he's nice," Amanda countered.

"Mandy, tell me something. Are you one of those people who tries to see something good in other people, no matter what low-life snakes they are?"

"Well, kinda, I guess."

"Then you're about to find out that there's nothin' good about Travis. Nothin'."

"You're wrong. That's all I have to say," Amanda told him. She left in a huff, went to her room, and slammed the door.

"What's with your sister?"

"Oh, she's all right. Don't worry about her. We have much bigger things to worry about." Then they decided to go to bed, too. Once Todd was securely under his covers he began thinking about a whole bunch of things all at once. There were the rustlers he'd seen on the very first night, the sheriff and his men, the conversation he'd overheard with his uncle, the guy in the old house, and now the tire tracks. If that didn't scare him, they were about to head out into open-county with danger behind every rock.

As he lay there alone in the darkness, Todd started having that achy, breaky, shaky, feeling again. He pulled the covers tightly up against his chin and drifted off to sleep. He started having some of the strangest dreams, but none of them made any sense. Around three o'clock in the morning he woke up hugging both of his pillows. All of his blankets were on the floor. *This is ridiculous,* he decided. He gathered up his covers off the floor, spread them over himself, and managed to go back to sleep.

At four o'clock he heard the warning bell, the signal that everyone going on the roundup had better get up. Todd knew his sister could sleep through an earthquake, so he went in to wake her. He saw that the light in Drew's room was already on. Before long they were standing outside with the others when Uncle Reid instructed everyone to get the horses.

Again the children picked out their same animals, and as before, someone had already put the saddles on them. They walked their horses back out to where the rest of the cowboys were gathering.

"Let's move out," their uncle ordered. It was really something to see. The sun was just beginning to show itself for a brand new day, but the sky was still mostly dark blue. Heading out the cowboys and horses looked like the black, paper cutouts Todd had seen artists make at the festivals his family went to in the city.

The horses made all sorts of funny sounds. Some of them made grinding noises as they chomped at the bit in their mouths. The horse's shoes made different sounds as they walked on dirt and rocks.

The air was cool and with each passing minute the sky became brighter. No one was talking. Todd thought most of the men were still asleep trusting their horses to stay on the trail. He thought it looked like a part of a circus parade.

After they had ridden for a couple of hours, the sun was fully up in the sky. It was getting warmer. Uncle Reid, who was at the front of the procession, held up his left hand and said, "Halt." The entire line of men and horses came to a stop. "It's breakfast time," he announced.

Each person dismounted and reached into his saddle-bag and selected the items he wanted for breakfast. It didn't take long to eat, but it was important to give their horses a rest. So it was a full thirty minutes before Uncle Reid announced, "Let's hit the trail. We'll be stopping later for lunch. Then it's on till nearly dusk. Hopefully we'll reach those who headed out yesterday . . . including Cookie and a great chow time tonight."

Everyone nodded when he mentioned Cookie. Then Uncle Reid gave the order, "Let's move it, people."

The day went by quickly for Todd. Everything was so new and exciting that he was surprised when it was time to stop for lunch. Amanda quickly joined him as Drew wondered off for a few minutes and then came over and sat down.

Todd was eager to get started again, but Drew told them it would be an hour before they headed out. Of course, Amanda had to ask why. Drew explained that the horses were getting plenty of rest because they had several hard days of work ahead. With that news, they lay on the grass and watched the clouds move across the sky. As they were getting ready to mount and head out, Todd noticed Travis talking secretly with one of the other ranch hands.

The afternoon was uneventful for the city-kids, they were

beginning to get tired of the new transportation. Riding horses was definitely different from riding in the back seat of their SUV. They were hurting in places they were too embarrassed to mention.

Amanda had made friends with some of the cowhands, and Todd didn't worry about her. He was much more interested in keeping his eye on Travis. He noticed that Drew was doing the same.

As the dusk was settling someone saw the camp site and passed the word along. No one complained because they had reached the end of the trail for the day. Cookie had everything ready. The three kids were starving, but so were some of the others.

After dinner, everyone had jobs to do to get camp ready. It took about an hour. By the time they were finished, it was completely dark. Cookie had a large fire built in the middle of the camp. As each person finished his job, he would make his way to the warmth and friendly glow of that blaze.

Todd felt safe with all the strong, rugged men in camp. If there really were any rustlers out there someplace, he knew nothing could happen to him. Then he heard a sound like nothing he had ever heard before.

"What . . . is . . . that?" he asked.

"That's just a pack of coyotes," one of the men answered. "They're bowlegged, good-for-nothin' varmints," he grumbled.

"I think that's the saddest sound I've ever heard," Amanda said with a whimper. "Do they look like that one in the cartoon that chases the Roadrunner?"

"Pretty close to that."

"What exactly is a coyote?" Todd asked.

"A kind of wild dog . . . smaller than a wolf, but they're very smart."

Todd thought for a minute. "How do you know they're smart?"

"Because in all the years people have tried to kill them off, they just keep comin' back stronger than ever," a cowboy answered. "The problem is they kill a lot of sheep."

"You mean they kill those sweet, adorable, little lambs?" Amanda questioned.

"Yes," Travis answered, "but we don't have any sheep on this ranch."

"How come?" Todd wanted to know.

"It's kind of a tradition. They say that cattle and sheep just don't mix. Actually, I think it's the ranchers that think guys who raise sheep are wimpy, and there isn't anything on this earth dumber than a sheep."

"That's not nice," Amanda scolded.

"Sorry there, little lady, but it's true. Did you know that if you had a bunch of sheep running together and the first one in line decided to jump off a cliff, the rest would follow him?"

"That *is* dumb," Todd said.

"Let's call it a night, people," Uncle Reid announced. "We got our work cut out for us in the morning."

Todd liked the way his uncle was in charge of everything.

The men did whatever he said, and they all seemed to like him, too, even Travis. Todd, Drew, and Amanda slithered into their sleeping bags.

"Hey Drew," Todd began, "can you explain what a round-up is exactly."

"Easy. We turn the animals out onto the range for months. Then the cows have their calves out here. Since they don't bring the little critters in to meet the family, we have to go out and meet them."

"That's it?"

"That's far from it. We have to put the mark of our ranch on every one we find. It's called a brand."

"I've read about that," Todd added. "You do it with fire and a hot iron, don't you."

"With some, yes."

"Doesn't that hurt the little babies?" Amanda asked.

"They have a pretty tough hide, but I suppose it can hurt. My dad's been experimenting with a different process. They're supposed to try it out tomorrow."

"What is it?"

"They call it freeze branding. Somebody can tell you all about it in the morning. It's pretty cool."

"Freeze branding is pretty cool. That's funny," Amanda laughed.

The camp began to quiet down. One man had to be on guard at all times, so several of the ranch hands took turns. The guard was also supposed to keep the fire going. Todd could already hear some of the other men snoring.

"Hey Drew?" Todd whispered.

"Yeah?" he answered with a yawn.

"This isn't the place where you take some of those rattlesnakes is it?"

"No, but they're out here all right."

"Do they come in and bother us if we're on the ground like this?" Amanda asked with a slight alarm in her voice.

"They can. Those things like to find a toasty place to sleep, and somebody snuggled in a warm sleeping bag is just about the right temperature."

"Drew," one of the men scolded. "Knock it off. You're scaring those kids."

"Well, it's true."

"Yeah, but it almost never ever happens."

"Almost never?" Todd questioned.

"Go to sleep," another cowboy told them.

Just as Todd was about to do that, he heard a very loud sound right next to his ear. He tried to ignore it, but it sounded exactly like those rattlers in the truck box. His heart began pounding like it wanted to jump right out of his chest and run into the hills.

He knew he wasn't supposed to make any sudden moves, so he slowly opened one eye, slightly turned his head, and then he saw it. He was looking face to face at Drew. What was Drew doing next to his head? In his hand, he held some kind of a noisemaker that sounded exactly like a rattlesnake.

Todd reached out and grabbed whatever it was from Drew's hand and flung it as far as he could. It just happened to land right in the middle of the giant campfire.

"Hey," Drew complained, "that thing cost almost twenty bucks. You owe me."

"*Owe* you? You're lucky I don't haul off and smack you one. Now go back to bed, and I hope you have a visitor waiting for you when you crawl in."

Todd laid flat on his back. The sky was darker here than anywhere he had ever lived. He began counting the stars, but there were so many of them in all shapes and sizes. Some were very bright and others were dim. They all seemed to twinkle like the little white lights on his Christmas tree back home. He had the hardest time shutting off his mind and going to sleep.

First, there was all that snoring. The fire made noise, his sister became restless as she started having a bad dream, and the coyotes were howling. Then, the thought of a snake sneaking silently into his sleeping bag in the middle of the night kept him awake until he couldn't stand it any more. Rustlers were the last thing on his mind. Finally, he too went to sleep like all the others except for the guards.

Chapter 12

While it was still dark, Todd heard voices. *It can't be morning yet*, he thought, *I'm still sleepy.* His eyes felt all blurry and it was difficult to focus on his watch at first. "Three o'clock," he whispered. Then he wondered, *What's going on anyway?*

"I saw some lights over that way, Mr. Brannon," a voice said.

"Give me the binoculars. Now where did you say?"

"Due south. Right on the horizon there." Todd could now see the men standing in the glow of the campfire. It was his uncle all right and one of the guards. He got out of his sleeping bag and crept nearer to them.

"What do you make of it, sir?"

"I'm not sure. Could be nothing, but I'm starting to see a pattern here. It all links up to some of the information the sheriff had."

"Got any ideas?"

"Not yet. We'll just need to tell the men to keep a sharp watch when we ride out in the morning."

Todd slinked back to his bedroll. As he crawled in, part of him loved the adventure and part of him was scared to death. *Sure glad I'm not out here all by myself,* he thought. The next thing he knew, six ATVs, like the kind his cousin owned came roaring into camp. The men driving them were dressed completely in black. Two of them drove back outside the camp circle, driving around and around so no one could leave. The others came to a stop in the center.

"Who's in charge here?" a scary man asked as he stood to his feet. He was bigger and meaner looking than anyone on the cattle drive. Todd knew they were really in trouble now.

"I said who's in charge here?"

"He is," Travis said in a gruff voice like Todd had never heard before. Todd watched helplessly as Travis brought Uncle Reid into the center of the ring. He had a lasso around his neck and Travis was pulling on him because Mr. Brannon didn't want to cooperate.

"We're taking *all* your cattle," the scary man threatened. "There ain't nothing none of you can do about it." He laughed an evil, thunderous laugh. The other men that were with him began laughing, too. It sounded like a terrible thunder just before a big storm.

Then Todd got an idea. If he could crawl quietly behind the big man, he figured he would be able to kick him in the back of the legs so he'd tumble into the fire. Slowly, oh so slowly, he began rolling in his sleeping bag, closer and closer to the fire until he was directly behind the biggest man he had ever seen.

He looked even bigger because he was standing up, and Todd was still down on the ground.

Todd turned himself around until his feet were right behind the man who continued laughing at the top of his voice. The sound of thunder roared louder and louder at the same time. Then suddenly, Todd began to kick like a punter in the NFL. But, as he did that, several of the cowboys from the ranch grabbed him and held his legs so he couldn't kick any more.

"Hey, cut that out. Let me go," he screamed. At the same time he started getting hotter because by now he was right next to the fire. He could smell his hair as the heat from that great blaze started to singe some of it.

"Todd, Todd," Uncle Reid comforted. "Get away from the flames before you catch yourself on fire." He continued shaking his nephew until he woke up. "Hurry, son, we have to get under cover, there's a big storm coming up the draw."

Now, Todd was really embarrassed. After all, it was his sister who was supposed to have the bad dreams and go sleepwalking. *At least I've only been sleep rolling,* he thought. Still he felt stupid to have made such a dope of himself in front of the whole camp. Cookie and some of the others had fixed up a shelter off both sides of the chuck wagon with large tarps. Todd scrambled under one of them as the first raindrops fell.

"Must have been *some* dream," Drew teased. Todd didn't answer.

The storm carried powerful winds that made the rain blow almost sideways instead of falling straight down to the ground. Plenty of rain was making it to the ground because water began rushing past Todd's feet. He found a place up on the wagon so he could get out of the mud. Then, as quickly as the storm had blown up, it stopped.

"Is that it?" he asked his cousin.

"Could be. They come and go like that sometimes out here."

Their uncle came slogging through the mud. He was wearing tall rubber boots, a yellow rain jacket, and a plastic cover over his wide cowboy hat. "Might as well get breakfast started, Cookie. We're not going back to bed."

"Tarnation!" Cookie protested. "I already got this here coffee brewing, but I can't cook anything till everybody gets off my wagon."

"Go ahead and serve the coffee when it's ready, then. We're camped on a pretty sandy spot. Most of the water will soak in soon."

Everyone honored Cookie's request and cleared away from the chuck wagon.

One of the cowboys at the back of the wagon asked, "So where are you kids from?"

"Illinois," Todd announced proudly.

"You're Drew's cousins, right?" asked another.

"That's right," Drew said.

"Now, I've got a question," Todd added.

"About what?" a cowboy, near the front of the wagon, asked.

"Before we came out here, I was reading a book about cattle rustling in the old days. I thought things like that and gunfights were just back in olden times. But now I keep hearing about rustlers on this ranch. What's going on?" When he finished his question he noticed Travis slipping out the back flap of the wagon. Then someone he couldn't see spoke up.

"It's pretty big business these days. You see, back in the times that your book told about, guys would ride in, steal a few cattle, and herd them off to *their* ranch. This happened especially in the spring when the new calves had been born, but they weren't branded yet. If no one could prove who owned them, then most likely the rustlers would be able to keep them. It's the only way a guy could build up a herd faster."

"But stealing is wrong," Amanda said.

"Look at it this way. We all work for Mr. Brannon. Our job for most of the year is to help him with his cattle. Now, if some other guys come to the ranch and suddenly start stealing animals, we'd lose our jobs. Mr. Brannon might even have to sell this place."

"That would be sad," Amanda said.

"It really would be, but that's the way things work. One person may spend the time and money to run a store, a restaurant, or a ranch. They plan to sell things so they can keep on doing whatever it is they're doing. Do you understand?"

"Yes, I think so."

"Today the rustlers operate a big business. They hit fast and they hit hard."

"How do they do it?" Todd asked.

"Small bands of them swoop into an area with pickup trucks, those all terrain vehicles, and trailers. They round up animals with their ATVs, run them into the trailers, and they're gone."

"Where do they go?" Amanda asked.

"I heard you might have seen one of their trucks and trailers on your way in here the other night."

"We might have. Do they always steal at night?"

"Most of them do, but if they think no one is watching, they'll try it any time, any place."

"So what about the trailer we saw?" Todd prodded.

"After they get all the animals they want, they make them get in the front of the trailer, close a gate, and drive the ATVs into the space that's left. The back gate is closed, even with the men still back there, and the pickup speeds to the staging area."

"Then what?"

"At that place there are big rigs waiting for them."

"Big rigs?"

"Eighteen wheelers. Semis. You know, those big trucks you always see on the highway. The animals are loaded in from all the smaller trailers. Everybody scatters and the big rigs speed off down the Interstate to sell the animals they stole. It's big business and big money."

"Couldn't they just work on a ranch like you guys do and have their own animals?" Todd asked.

"Well, any time there is stuff to steal, there will always

be people who are willing to steal it because they're too lazy to work and get it honestly. Cattle look like walking dollar bills to a rustler. And there are rustlers, not just here, but in Canada, Africa, Australia . . . anyplace where people raise animals."

That troubled Todd because there was still something he hadn't told anyone, not even his sister. It was starting to bother him a lot. Back home, he and his family didn't go to church, but he knew the difference between right and wrong. Those friends he hung around with at school weren't exactly some of the best.

"That's it guys . . . and lady," Uncle Reid called out, as he tipped his hat to Amanda. "Time to break camp while Cookie makes our breakfast."

Todd jumped down from the wagon and walked over to his uncle. "You got a minute?" he asked.

"For you, all the time you need, Todd." They began walking up toward some jagged rocks.

"If I tell you something, do you promise not to tell my dad?" he asked.

"Now that depends on what it is. Some things you have to tell no matter what they are."

"Well, when I was back home, me and some of my friends started going into stores and stealing stuff."

"Todd!" his sister scolded as she walked up to where they were sitting. "I'm telling Dad."

"Listen, Amanda. Stealing is a very serious thing, but admitting it is even more important," her uncle said.

"So that's why you and your friends wear the Pittsburgh

Steelers jerseys?"

"Yeah, it's kind of a private joke," Todd said.

"A dumb joke if you ask me. It isn't even spelled right."

"But, what should I do?" Todd groaned.

"The best thing would be to tell your dad. If I know my brother, at least he's a fair man. He'll understand, and I think he'll want to help."

"Then, that's it?"

"Not at all. The next thing you have to do is tell your friends it was wrong and you aren't going to do it any more. After that, you should pray and tell God you're sorry."

"I don't know too much about God."

"He's one of my very best friends, Todd. If you want to talk about Him any time, you just let me know."

"I'll think about it. Are those all the things I have to do?"

"I'm afraid not because the hardest one is still coming."

"What's that?"

"You have to go back to any store where you stole something, find the owner, and tell him you're sorry. Then you need to figure a way to give back what you stole."

A little confused, Todd said, "I ate some of it."

"In that case, you need to pay for what you ate, or make an agreement with the owner so he's happy. You might have to work a little around the store."

"Kind of like Travis?"

"Now wait a minute! What do you think you know about Travis?"

"Oh, nothing."

"Did you want to add lying to stealing?"

"I promised not to tell."

"That's okay. I have a pretty good idea. The important thing is no matter what you think you know, from the day Travis came to work for me, I couldn't ask for a more honest, hard-working person. I'd even be proud to have him as a son."

"You would?"

"He's made some mistakes, big ones, and now he's paying for them. But I'd trust that guy no matter what. You can, too."

Todd thought about that for a moment. It was a bit confusing because of what Drew had told him and what they saw in the old house. He still wondered why Travis sneaked out of the wagon when they started talking about rustlers.

"I'll talk with you later if that's okay," Todd said.

"Fine with me."

Chapter 13

Todd walked quietly back to camp. He didn't like the fact that he'd had such bad thoughts about Travis. Sure, he'd stolen things that were a lot bigger and worth a lot more money than Todd ever had, but at the same time he knew stealing was stealing no matter how big or how small. His grandmother had taught him that.

He noticed his uncle going toward the chuck wagon. When he got there, he took out a large satellite telephone and punched in a number.

"Hello, sheriff? This is Reid. One of the guards saw some strange lights early this morning." He listened a moment, then continued, "They were straight south, in the area where we came through the other night, I think." After listening for about a minute he spoke again, "We'll do that. You might want to get that bird in the air, though, because, with the rain we got this morning, all the tracks will be washed out." A few seconds later he concluded, "Right, I will, and you take care, too." After that he turned the phone off and placed it back in the box on the wagon.

Todd's uncle gathered all the men in the middle of camp. "We're going to move out in teams of six. The children won't count in that number, so they can go with whatever group they want to. But kids, I want you to stay together."

"We will," all three promised.

"Here's what I want the rest of you to do. The main reason we're out here today is to bring in the spring strays, brand the ones that need it, and turn them back out. But there's an added chore this time."

"What's that, boss?"

"There are definitely rustlers in the area. Jim Jenson, who owns the place just west of my ranch, lost nearly forty head last night, and the sheriff told me this morning that other reports are coming in. This morning we saw some strange lights to the south. If you keep your eyes open, you might be the ones to help catch these guys."

Now Todd was excited again. At least he would be protected with all the cowboys around. Plus, he knew the sheriff and all his men would be hunting, too. Todd and Drew decided they should join the group Travis was riding with. Since Uncle Reid said to stay together, Amanda didn't have any choice.

"Let's move out," their leader said. They rode together for nearly an hour but didn't see any animals. Todd hoped his group wouldn't be the only one that didn't find any.

"Should be easy today," one of the cowboys suggested. "After all that rain, any tracks we see will be fresh."

The search party began riding up a long sloping hillside. To make it easier on the horses, they went in a zigzag pattern instead of straight up. Each team leader had a two-way radio so he could talk to someone at the base camp. Todd's group finally made it to the top of the hill. From there he could see the entire surrounding countryside. There were beautiful rock formations that looked as if the early morning rain had washed them off especially for him to see. The colors were light and dark browns with patches of green mixed in. He also saw small streams, trees, and rocks everywhere.

The leader took out his binoculars and began a visual sweep of the landscape.

"There should be a few down there someplace," he reported. "Our air search plotted this as one of the main areas." After looking a little longer, Travis asked, "Mind if I take a look?"

Todd and Drew glanced at each other, raised their eyebrows, and slightly nodded their heads.

Todd looked out then suddenly said, "I just saw something move down there."

"Where?" Travis asked.

"Just beyond that ridge."

"Todd, don't scare me like that," Amanda warned.

"No, really. I saw something . . . or someone."

"I think we should ride down there and take a closer look," Travis suggested.

"Guess so. Let's move on out, men and lady."

"Thank you," Amanda said.

Riding down the hill was easier on the horses, so they made pretty much a straight path. After reaching the flat land again, the group headed off in the direction where Todd had pointed from up top. About two hours later their leader raised his hand. "Hold up," he said.

He jumped down from his horse and along with Travis made his way over to a spot near some tall grass. Most of the men stayed on their horses, but the children wanted to see what was happening. They each slipped off their horse and walked toward Travis and their leader.

"Tracks all right," Travis said. "Cattle *and* vehicles. And look here. You can see some boot prints, too."

As the children walked up to a clump of tall grass, Travis got down on one knee, took off his glove, and felt the boot print with his hand. "No doubt about it. They've been here, and not long ago."

"Rustlers?" Todd asked.

"Yup."

"Boy, howdy," Drew exclaimed as he and the cousins crouched down by some other tracks next to a clump of tall weeds and grass.

No sooner did they get there than Todd heard that unmistakably scary, sickening sound of a full-grown rattlesnake.

"Stop it, Drew. That's not funny."

"It ain't me," Drew responded. The two boys slowly turned in time to see Amanda looking white as house paint and standing as rigid as the petrified wood Todd had put in his pocket at the abandoned ranch.

"Don't you *move*," Travis warned. "Don't even twitch." In an instant he lunged toward Amanda, wrapped his arms tightly around her, and pulled her from danger. But as he did that, the snake struck, burying its fangs deep in the back of Travis' leg just above his boot line. As Travis and Amanda came crashing to the ground, Travis yelled, "He bit me! That thing really bit me!"

No one noticed the snake as it slithered away. They were too worried about Travis. They didn't even look to see if there were any more snakes.

Right away Amanda began crying uncontrollably. "Mister," she asked, "is he going to die?"

"I heard you're supposed to take a knife, cut an X over the bites, and suck out the poison," Todd suggested.

"A lot of people think that," their leader told them, "but it's wrong."

"Then, what'll we do?" Todd cried.

"Drew," the man yelled, "get on my radio and call base camp. Tell them we have a snake bite out here." Drew took the radio and began, "Base, base, this is Drew. Over."

"Drew, this is Cookie. Whatcha need?"

"It's awful, Cookie, just awful. Travis got bitten by a really big rattler." Then he started to cry.

"Calm down, son," the cook comforted. "Your leader knows what to do. Just follow his instructions."

"Give me the radio, Drew," their leader said. "Cookie, I'm going to give you some coordinates on my map here. Get on the satellite phone and relay the information to the sheriff. He's supposed to have a state police chopper working the area today. See if you can arrange a pickup and tell him we found tracks and may have seen somone."

"Roger that."

"And get somebody on a horse pronto with the antidote."

"I'm handing it to him right now."

"Thanks, man."

The leader turned to the children and Travis. "The first thing we need to do is keep him laying on the ground. Travis, buddy, try to be as calm and quiet as you can. You're lucky the bite is so low on your leg."

"Why?" Todd asked.

"Because the farther from his heart the better."

"I don't want to know why that is," Amanda whimpered. She took Travis' hand and softly stroked it. With tears streaming down both cheeks, and choking on the words she said, "Travis, I was the one who should have been bitten . . . not you. Thank you for getting me out of the way."

Travis struggled for the words but managed to say, "You're welcome, sweetheart. There was no way I could let that dangerous thing get any closer to you."

"But," she took a deep breath with tears continuing to stream down her face, "you didn't have to do it."

"Yeah, I did."

"Come on, Travis, lay still so I can get to work on you," the leader said. He took out a big knife from a leather sheath on his belt. The knife had a long gleaming blade with a silver and black handle.

"I thought you weren't supposed to cut him," Todd protested.

"I'm not, but I can't get to his wound unless I cut his pant leg first." He slipped the blade between Travis' jeans and the top of his boot. Then he began cutting a slit in the material all the way up to his knee. He stabbed the knife into the dirt then reached up and pulled open the fabric.

There, staring back at them were two reddish-purple marks on Travis' leg.

"Will you look at that? He really tagged you man. Just keep calm, Travis. Help is on the way. You need to take off rings, your watch, and any chains you might have around your neck."

"Amanda," Travis asked, "could you help me?" Tenderly she removed his watch and a bracelet that had his name on it.

"My neck, too."

She reached around his collar and her fumbling fingers found a chain. Amanda pulled on it until something at the end of the chain flopped out. She held a beautiful gold cross, gleaming in the sunlight. Amanda slipped the chain over his head, and then put everything in her pocket.

"Next, I have to clean the wound area." The leader took some water from his canteen and a cloth out of his saddlebag. "I keep a small bar of soap in my snake kit," he told them. With these things he was able to clean all around the bite marks. "We have to keep the bite part just below the level of your heart,

Travis, so I'm going to turn your legs a little down the hill."

Todd could hear a horse coming up like it was ten lengths ahead in the Kentucky Derby. Looking closer he noticed his uncle was the rider. Without even letting the horse come to a stop, Uncle Reid leaped off and came running to where Travis was sprawled out in the dirt.

"How you doin', man?" he asked in a caring voice.

"Okay, I think."

"It's all my fault," Amanda said, and then she began sobbing again.

"Don't worry, darlin'. He's going to be just fine." Their uncle took a small box out of his leather vest pocket. He opened it to reveal a syringe and three small glass bottles.

"What's that stuff?" Todd asked in wonder.

"Antidote. This little bottle here is going to make our friend all better." He took a shield off the needle, stuck it into the soft top of the bottle and drew out most of the liquid. When he pulled it back out, he turned the shiny needle straight into the air. Then he pushed on the other end until a small amount of the liquid squirted into the air. The droplets looked like a string of diamonds as the sun shone brightly through each drop.

"Now this is going to hurt a little, my friend, so just hang in there." He plunged the needle into Travis' flesh, and when he did, it reminded Todd of how the snake had sunk his two needle-like fangs in there, too. Todd got a quivering, lightheaded feeling all over. He stood to his feet, stumbled for two or three steps, and nearly fainted. As he sank back to the ground, he threw up all over the bushes.

"It's okay," Uncle Reid assured him. "That's happened to a lot of guys bigger than you."

Drew went over to his cousin and asked, "You gonna be okay?"

"Could you get me some water?" he coughed.

The faint sound of a helicopter could be heard in the distance. Todd raised himself up on one elbow so he could watch it come in. Soon it was hovering directly above them. Todd's uncle gave signals with his arms that must have made sense to the pilot because the chopper began a slight turn, drifted to one side, and lowered gently to the ground. The shock waves from its massive, spinning blades hurt Todd's ears, and the dust started getting in his eyes.

"Let's get him to the ranch," Todd's uncle ordered the pilot, "and then we can transfer him to my plane. I'll fly him to the city from there."

"We can take him on in Mr. Brannon."

"You could, but you guys need to stay on the trail of those rustlers. They can't be far off now. I think the rain may have trapped them someplace."

"I think I saw one of them over there," Todd said as he pointed toward the opening of a canyon.

"But sir," the pilot protested.

"Don't argue with me. Just do as I tell you," Uncle Reid snapped back. Several of the others from the team had gotten off their horses and now helped lay Travis down in the back of the helicopter as Uncle Reid joined him. "All right, men. Stay here and watch the canyon."

In minutes the chopper was back in the air, speeding toward the ranch. Todd watched until it finally faded from sight.

"Is he going to be okay?" Amanda whimpered.

"I hope so," their leader said. "I sure do hope so."

Chapter 14

A couple hours later their team leader got a call over his radio to return to camp.

"What for?" Todd asked. "We know right where they are."

"Orders are orders." The leader answered.

When the group reached camp again, Todd noticed some of the men had built a corral using a place with steep rocks on three sides. At the end they constructed a temporary fence out of logs and brush. In the middle was an opening with a gate made out of more logs and sticks. A few calves were already inside.

"How did you get them in there?" Todd asked.

"It's easy," Drew said. "Cows are pretty dumb. They just go wherever we tell them to."

"So now what?" Amanda asked.

"Now we have to put our brand on them."

"Brand?"

"Our mark. Here, I'll show you." He picked up an iron rod with a pattern on one end. "Look here. We use an 'RR'."

Todd studied the letters for a moment. "I get it, Reid

Ryder, right?"

"That's it."

"My favorite brand is the bar-b-cue," Amanda snickered.

"Mine's the golden arches," Todd added.

"I thought branding could hurt them," Amanda said.

"It does some. So my dad is trying this other way I told you about. One of the guys will show you."

Since their uncle wasn't around to explain it, another cowboy offered to try. "It's called freeze branding."

"Freeze, like ice?" Todd asked.

"Yes, it's a lot like that. Instead of making the iron hot and burning the skin, we make it cold and freeze the area."

"What does that do?"

"Well, it kind of burns too but not in the same way."

"Does it hurt them?" Amanda asked.

"I'm sure it does some but nothing like the hot one."

"I think I like that better. Poor little calfy, wafy," she sighed.

Drew spoke up, "Travis told me a branding joke once. Wanna hear it?"

"Why not?" Todd groaned.

"Seems this guy owned a ranch, and he was telling another man in town about his place.

"'What's the name of your ranch?' the other man asked.

"'I call her the Flying R, double S, Circle B, Bar U, Box D, Triple W, ABC Delicious Ranch,' he said proudly. 'So I went and had the blacksmith make me up the biggest, baddest brand in the territory.'

"The other man thought for a second and then asked, 'So how many head you running out on your place?'

"'Oh, we don't have any cattle," he told him sadly.

"'How come?'

"'Seems none of them could survive the brand.'"

Drew started laughing. "Travis loves to tell that one."

"Do you see that area next to the fence?" The cowboy pointed over to a sort of double fence.

"Yes," Todd answered.

"We run them in through there, one by one. First, one cowboy takes clippers and cuts the hair in the area we plan to brand. While he's doing that, the iron is getting freezing cold. When the calf comes to the next station, someone washes the area with a special liquid. From there he walks to a spot where he's held tight because we have to hold the iron on the skin for at least two minutes . . . longer if we can."

"What if you don't keep it on?"

"Then we have to do it all over again because this brand takes longer to leave its mark."

"Then what?"

"That's all there is to it. The calf gets to run back to its mother, and they can have a cow party for all I care."

"But the brand. . . . if you don't burn it, how can anyone see it afterwards?"

"With a freeze brand you can see it faintly right away because the skin swells up some. In about twenty days, the new hairs grow back white in the shape of the brand. Then the design stays white from then on."

"So your mark is to help keep other people from stealing your animals?"

"Yes. We have to register our mark. Any buyer, if he's honest, will look for the mark to make sure the animal isn't stolen. Of course, there are some dishonest buyers, too. There isn't much you can do about that. But some people are experimenting by putting computer chips under the skin of their cattle so they can track them electronically."

"That sounds pretty cool," Todd commented.

For the rest of the day they continued moving cattle through the chute they'd made. When it got dark, they returned to their campsite where the smell of dinner filled the air.

"Yum," Drew said.

"Yum double," Todd added.

"Yum times a hundred," Amanda countered.

After supper, it was time to sit around the fire again. Most of the conversation was about Travis. Several of the guys were calling him a hero. Amanda leaned over and whispered to Todd that she thought so, too.

"Do you think he'll be okay?" she asked.

One of the men answered, "We did everything we could. He won't die. I can tell you that. But he'll need to be in the hospital for a few days."

Todd wasn't sure, but he thought he could hear the helicopter again. Since it was so dark, he wondered if it could find them. Soon it was hovering right above their site. One of the men got on the radio and gave instructions for a night landing. This time, after it settled to the ground, the pilot turned off the engine and the huge blades slowly came to a stop. When the doors slid open, Todd watched as his uncle and the sheriff stepped out.

Uncle Reid walked over to the children. "I've got good news," he told them. "Travis is going to be okay."

"Can we go see him?" Amanda asked.

"Maybe in a day or so. The sheriff has even bigger news, and he needs all of you to pay close attention."

"We've located a place we think is the loading area where the rustlers are. It's the spot you pointed out, Todd."

Drew patted him on the shoulder.

"Because of the weather, it looks like they can't get out yet, so my men are moving into position now for a mission, on my signal, at first light."

"This is really exciting," Todd whispered to his sister.

"What I need you men to do is ride your horses out to the west and take up a position along a line that runs north – south. My men will be waiting with their four-wheel drive trucks to the east. We think the rustlers might make a run for it, and they should run smack dab into my officers."

"Do you think the rustlers will have weapons?" a man asked.

"They might, but it won't matter to you."

"How's that?"

"Well, you'll be about a half mile away from their position. I'm going to give several of you signal flare guns and to the others lots of fireworks. After we set everything off, those poor guys will think the entire US Army is after them."

Amanda giggled at that thought.

"They can't drive out of there with all the mud, so I expect they'll turn tail and try to run out on foot, right into the waiting arms of my guys who'll probably have great big grins on their faces by that time."

Before the sun came up everyone was in position. All the radios that the cowboys had, and the ones in all the police trucks, and the helicopter radio were tuned to the same frequency. When the sheriff gave his signal, practically the whole world was going to hear it. The children got to go out to an area that wasn't too dangerous. Drew's dad fixed them up with a radio and binoculars. What a show they had!

From all the radio transmissions, Todd imagined he was watching a major military operation like the commanding general from a high hill. The sheriff gave his signal, and the children watched as Uncle Reid's men were on the move. In the distance they saw the flares, and then the Roman Candles were fired. Over the radio they could hear a lot of yelling and firecrackers. Then only silence.

"What happened?" Todd asked.

"Now we just wait," Drew said.

They waited, and they waited, and then they waited some more until finally it happened. Over the radio a voice clearly reported, "We got 'em . . . all of them!"

Todd watched as several men were herded out of the canyon like cattle. He could hardly wait till someone came back to camp to report what happened. It was nearly noon before the faint sound of the helicopter could be heard again. It soon settled in the grass not far from camp. As Drew's father climbed out, the children dashed over to him with a million questions.

"We could see the whole thing!"

"What happened?"

"How many were there?"

"What did they look like?"

"Is anybody hurt?" On and on the questions kept coming. Uncle Reid finally held up both of his hands and pleaded, "One at a time, please."

"How's Travis?" Amanda asked sweetly. "Can we go see him?"

"First, the surprise was total. They were exactly where you said, Todd. The rustlers ran right into the sheriff's men like he thought they would. They left all their trucks, trailers, and equipment, and just ran for their lives."

"Why didn't they try to drive out?" Drew asked.

"They were all set up in a box canyon. Todd, Amanda, you probably don't know what a box canyon is, but it's a place with only one way in and out. We call it a box because it's closed on three sides. At the far end of the canyon is where they had everything hidden."

"But, I still don't understand why they didn't make a run

for it with the trucks," Drew continued.

"Well, between the end of the canyon and the only way out of that place water from the storm had collected into a large pond. Most of it had settled into the ground, but there were about three feet of mud left behind."

"Wow," Amanda said.

"Those guys were lucky to make it out on foot. But that's not the best part."

"It isn't?" Todd asked.

"No, sir, it isn't. At the back of the canyon we found over two thousand head of cattle that had been stolen from all over this area."

Drew just let out a long, high-pitched whistle.

"See, they had several problems. First, they couldn't get anything heavy out . . . including any of the animals . . . because they would have just sunk right in. Second, the big rigs couldn't get out either. They had cleared a dirt road, all the way out to route 59 and then covered it over with branches and brush. If Todd hadn't seen one of them, and if the mud wasn't there, all two thousand head would be rolling down the Interstate by now."

The sheriff walked up and added, "It was one of the most sophisticated, high-tech operations we've ever busted in these parts. I've never recovered so many cattle at one time."

The children listened in silence.

"Drew, your dad tells me it was Travis and your group that helped crack this thing wide open."

"We did? How?"

"The truth is, Amanda there is the one who should get all the credit."

Her face turned bright red, and she tried to hide behind her brother. "Mandy? What did she do?" Todd asked.

"When that old snake decided to take a bite out of her, you all were looking at some tracks. Am I right?"

"Yes, we were, but…"

"After you pointed out where you thought you'd seen someone and Drew's dad called for the chopper, my guy flew right over the box canyon on his way out. Actually, if you hadn't stopped to look at the tracks you discovered, chances are you'd have run right up on those rustlers."

That made one of those cold, shivering, shaking feelings Todd hated so much, come rolling through his bones. "I don't think I would have liked that at all," he said.

"Well, this way it all worked out for the best, except for the criminals. Those boys are looking at some serious jail time, and the county gets to keep all their stuff. Plus, we found the records that gave us details of the entire operation. At this very moment, Federal Marshals are making their arrests in Cheyenne, Sheridan, and Casper."

That name made Amanda giggle again.

"We've even found the main guy all the way down in Denver. I'm telling you, you kids are going to be big news around these parts for a long, long time."

Chapter 15

Todd wondered how he could ever return to his dull life back in the city. To him it seemed like Wyoming was the place to be.

Drew, Amanda, and Todd had been taken back to the ranch early because ranchers from all over the area had to go to the box canyon and identify their cattle. Now it made sense to Todd, more than ever, why animals needed to be marked.

Back at the bunkhouse there was time for a hot shower. It felt good to put on clean clothes again. Todd and his sister were still in their rooms while Drew flipped the satellite channels. Then suddenly he hollered, "You guys. Come quick!"

Todd and his sister ran out to see what he wanted.

"I found this news channel and the story about capturing all those rustlers is on."

"It is?" Amanda shrieked.

"Shhh!"

An announcer began, "And from our Wyoming bureau, one of the most bizarre stories this reporter has witnessed in over twenty years of broadcasting." He went on to list the number of men captured, the large number of animals, and seizure of vehicles and equipment. Then, right in the middle of the report, Amanda said, "I wonder if Travis knows about all this?"

"Did you ask your dad when we could go see him?" Todd asked.

"Oh, yeah, I forgot to tell you. As soon as he gets back, we're going in the plane down to the hospital in Cheyenne."

"Oh, goodie," Amanda said, as she hugged herself, and jumped up and down.

The next day they were all gathered around the hospital bed where their new, best friend lay.

"Are you going to die?" Todd's sister asked.

Travis just laughed, "I don't think so. The doc tells me I'll probably walk with a limp from now on, but that's better than being buzzard bait."

The children laughed . . . except for Amanda. "I'm sorry I made that snake bite you," she said almost in a whisper as she choked back her tears.

"Don't you think a thing about it. I'd do it all over again if I had to."

"You would?"

"Without even thinking about it."

"But why?"

"Your uncle has been teaching me some important lessons since I started working on his ranch. Did you know I'm supposed to be in prison right now?"

"Yes," she answered, too embarrassed to look into his eyes.

"You knew that, huh? Drew, did you tell them?"

"Yes, I'm sorry."

"Well, I'm not. I mean, I'm sorry for the bad things I've done, but the truth is I'm just as bad as those men the sheriff caught, and them guys will all be going to jail."

"But, why don't you have to?" Todd asked softly.

"I think I can explain it this way. I did something wrong. No doubt about it. But then your uncle, well, he decided to pay for it. Not only did he pay for it, he gave me a place where I could live from then on. He told me God did something like that, too, and because of what God did I get to live in Heaven forever. All I gotta do is believe it, and I sure do."

By now everyone in the room was crying, even the nurse and the doctor.

"So," Amanda stammered. "You kind of did the same thing for me when you pushed me out of the way and that mean old snake chomped its poison into your leg."

Travis thought about her words for a very long time. Then a tear slowly began to form in his eye. "Sweetheart, I never thought about it like that until just now. Yeah, it was kind of like that, wasn't it? See how much a person can change if he just gets a chance."

Now there wasn't a person in the room who didn't need an entire box of tissue.

Even big, Uncle Reid wiped away tears and said, "That's the way it works. We do wrong, but someone paid for it. All we have to do is believe."

Todd tugged at his uncle's shirtsleeve and pulled him toward the door. "Can I talk to you for a minute, in private?"

"Sure."

The two of them went out into the waiting area at the end of the hall. Todd took a deep breath. He was glad to see no one else was sitting there right then. He and his uncle sat down in the corner on two purple chairs with light colored wood armrests.

"Uncle Reid," he began, "there's a bunch of stuff I don't know yet, and I've been doin' a lot of thinking. But I think I want to do right. I don't want to steal things anymore with the guys I've been runnin' with."

"That's a good start."

"When I get home, I want to ask my dad if we can start going to church."

"Todd, that's something I have been praying about for a long, long time."

"I'll go back to every store and tell them what I did. It'll be the hardest thing I've ever done, but I'm going to do it."

"Wonderful. If you have any questions along the way, any questions at all, you just give your Uncle Reid a call on the phone and we'll talk it out if it's all right with your dad. Okay?"

Todd leaned over and gave his uncle a big hug. "It's a deal." Then they went in and joined the others.

"Hey, Todd," Drew said. "You're just in time for one of Travis' stupid jokes."

"Great. Which one?"

With a wide grin, Travis began, "There was this baby rattlesnake playing around outside, when he suddenly slithered, screaming at the top of his voice, 'Mommy, Mommy!' His mother quickly came outside to see what was wrong. 'Mommy,' he said, 'Are we poisonous?' 'Why, yes we are, sweetie. Why do you ask?' 'Oh no, because I just bit my tongue.'"

Now the room that had been full of tears erupted into uncontrolled laughter. It seemed to make everyone feel better.

"Travis," Amanda said. "Can I tell you a secret?"

"Sure. What is it?"

"Well, we thought you were trying to help the rustlers."

"Me? Why is that?"

"Because you seemed to sneak around all the time, and then. . . ."

"Then what?"

Now Todd couldn't help it, he just blurted out, "That was you in the old, abandoned ranch house. I know it was. I saw you, and your name was on some papers upstairs."

"I was hoping you didn't know just then."

"Why not?" Drew asked.

"Because when you kids rode up, I was writing down some map coordinates to help the sheriff catch those rustlers."

"You were?" Todd asked in wonder.

"Uh huh. From that upstairs window, I had a clear view of the whole valley. Since the sheriff knew all about my past, he figured I probably could still think like a rustler. You know what they say, once a rustler always a rustler." Then he looked at Uncle Reid and winked.

"So I was the forward lookout for the whole operation. We knew we were closing in."

"Then the snake," Amanda reminded him.

"Yes, the snake. But by then it was too late to stop. Then with Todd's sharp eye we were able to pinpoint exactly where they were hiding. I just didn't get to enjoy the big show."

"Sorry you missed it," Amanda told him.

"Me, too," he sighed. "Me, too."

"We gotta go home in a few days, Travis," Todd reminded him.

"I know, and I'm going to miss my two young city slickers. You kids should come out here for a visit every year."

"You'll have to talk to my dad about that," Todd said.

"I think after you get back home, he's going to want to come out, too," Uncle Reid added.

"Don't be too sure," Amanda sighed, "cause when my mom finds out about all the stuff that's happened to us, she's not going to let me out of the house till I'm fifty." Travis and the others laughed.

"Hey, Drew," Todd said. "Wonder if you could come visit us in the city this summer?"

"I think that could be arranged."

"You think so, Dad?"

"Sure, I do."

They would have stayed longer, but the nurse in charge

of the whole floor where Travis was staying came into the room and ordered everyone out. Before they left, though, Todd and Amanda gave Travis a big hug.

"Now you make sure when you get out of this place," Todd ordered, "that there's no limping. You got that?"

"Yes, sir," Travis answered with a smile.

Amanda got right up close to Travis' ear and whispered something. Then they both got tears in their eyes all over again.

When everyone left the room, Todd whispered to her in the hallway, "What did you tell him?"

"I told him thank you for saving me, and that I would never forget it, ever."

"Me, neither," Todd said. "From now on, I'm going to be different."

He put his arm around his sister, and she did the same to him as they walked out into the sunshine and headed back to the ranch.

- The End -